"Is there something else you need?" Aiden asked.

"As a matter of fact, there is" came Maddie's bright response. "We'll need a canoe."

"Sure—"

"And a coach."

Aiden stared at Maddie. She didn't mean *him*. But the adorable dimple in her cheek clearly said that yes, she did.

"It would be a conflict of interest," Aiden argued. "I *designed* the course."

"You'd be the boys' instructor." Maddie smiled. "You don't have to go out on the river with them."

Except that Aiden never stood on the shoreline. He used the clipboard to check off names, and the rest of the lesson took place on the river.

He glanced at the teenagers.

They needed a coach…and he needed one more chance to change everyone's minds about him.

"All right, then. Come back tomorrow at eight. In the morning."

"They'll be here," Maddie promised.

Aiden unleashed a slow smile. "And so will you."

Kathryn Springer is a lifelong Wisconsin resident. Growing up in a "newspaper" family, she spent long hours as a child plunking out stories on her mother's typewriter and hasn't stopped writing since. She loves to write inspirational romance because it allows her to combine her faith in God with her love of a happy ending.

Books by Kathryn Springer

Love Inspired

Castle Falls

The Bachelor Next Door
The Bachelor's Twins
The Bachelor's Perfect Match

Mirror Lake

A Place to Call Home
Love Finds a Home
The Prodigal Comes Home
Longing for Home
The Promise of Home
Making His Way Home

Visit the Author Profile page at Harlequin.com for more titles.

The Bachelor's Perfect Match

Kathryn Springer

Recycling programs for this product may not exist in your area.

ISBN-13: 978-1-335-50943-7

The Bachelor's Perfect Match

This edition published by arrangement with Love Inspired Books.

www.Harlequin.com

Printed in U.S.A.

O give thanks unto the Lord, for he is good:
for his mercy endureth for ever.
—*Psalms* 107:1

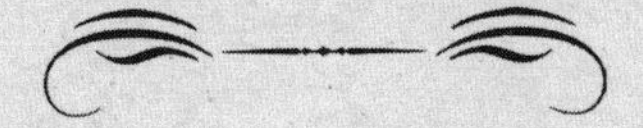

To Kayla
For being a wonderful first reader and friend!

Chapter One

At nine o'clock on Monday morning, Maddie Montgomery brewed a cup of Earl Gray tea and opened the Castle Falls Library, ready for another quiet, ordinary day.

And then someone dropped a pirate off at her door.

A slightly disheveled pirate in flannel and faded denim, wearing a rakish patch over one eye and brandishing an aluminum crutch instead of a cutlass.

Although Aiden Kane, the youngest of the three Kane brothers, somehow managed to make the *slightly disheveled* part look good.

Through the narrow, two-inch gap that separated the poetry section from the biographies, Maddie watched Aiden limp past the circulation desk, each strike of his crutch against the hardwood floor fracturing the peaceful silence in the room. He lurched to a stop a few feet from where she stood and lifted his head to look around.

Fortunately, the bookcases that shielded Maddie from view also muffled the gasp that slipped from her lips.

Mottled bruises ranging in color from pale ochre to deep mauve bloomed on his jaw, reminding Maddie of the abstract painting above the fireplace in the conference room. A sling cradled the cast on Aiden's left arm, and the bulky outline of a bandage distorted one leg of his jeans, making his knee appear double its normal size.

Maddie knew he'd been injured in an accident, but she hadn't actually seen the extent of those injuries until now.

In a community the size of Castle Falls, which didn't bother with a Neighborhood Watch program because everyone kept a close watch on their neighbors anyway, Aiden had been the main topic of conversation over the past week. According to the rumors, his pickup truck had left the road, sailed over the ditch and rolled several times before landing upside down—a hair's breadth away from a towering white pine that had planted its roots in the soil of Michigan's Upper Peninsula long before the town founders.

Aiden had a reputation for being a bit of a daredevil, so no one seemed surprised the accident had happened. Actually, based on the whispered comments Maddie had overheard in the reading nook, people were more surprised it hadn't happened *sooner.*

Maddie studied the marks on Aiden's handsome face, her stomach turning a slow cartwheel when she considered what the outcome might have been if his pickup had actually connected with that tree.

Aiden and his two older brothers, along with their adoptive mom, Sunni Mason, ran Castle Falls Outfitters a few miles outside town. When Aiden wasn't testing the canoes the family built and sold, he hired out his services as an instructor and guide. From what Maddie heard, the man spent more time on the river than he did on land.

And it showed.

He was healthy and outgoing and strong…and, to be honest, more than a little intimidating to a girl who would have happily laid claim to even *one* of those three things.

Aiden reached up to bat at a swatch of black hair that had slipped over his eye, and Maddie heard an audible *thunk* when the cast connected with his forehead. For some reason that small but sweetly vulnerable gesture, coupled with Aiden's quiet huff of frustration, made Maddie forget her own insecurities.

She straightened the collar of her black-and-white houndstooth dress and stepped out from behind the bookcase.

"Good morning."

Aiden pivoted toward her, and the tip of his crutch caught the edge of the rug that divided the aisle from the children's area. Maddie had never regarded it as a potential hazard until Aiden began to teeter. He tried to steady himself, and Maddie automatically reached out to do the same.

The muscles in Aiden's biceps, sculpted from hours spent paddling canoes and doing other outdoorsy things, contracted beneath her fingertips.

Suddenly, he didn't look so vulnerable anymore. He didn't look like the Aiden whom Maddie saw at New Life Fellowship on Sunday mornings, either. The one with the mischievous blue eyes and a smile that charmed every female between the ages of one and one hundred as he sauntered into the sanctuary.

Maybe because he wasn't smiling at all.

Maddie let go.

"Can I help you find something?" She tried not to stare at the jagged red scratches that fanned out from the gauze bandage over Aiden's left eye like cracks on a windowpane.

"No. I'm...waiting for someone."

Well, that explained a lot. His presence, for starters. In the five years since Maddie had taken Mrs. Whitman's place as head librarian, she couldn't remember Aiden ever once setting foot through the door of the library.

"The chairs by the window are pretty comfortable." Maddie pointed to the reading nook in the corner. "And it happens to be prime real estate because it's located right next to the coffeepot."

Maddie had purposely set up the area to resemble a

living room. Leather chairs with wide arms and generous laps circled the glass-topped coffee table. An oak buffet that had once belonged to Maddie's maternal grandmother had been converted into a beverage station, the drawers containing everything from packages of tea to colorful, hand-stamped bookmarks.

All the regular patrons gravitated there, and the tourists who popped in during the summer months seemed impressed that a small-town library offered a quiet retreat as well as a wide variety of books.

Aiden didn't look impressed.

"Do you work here…?" He stopped, clearly struggling, and his brows dipped together in a frown.

For a moment, Maddie wondered if Aiden had suffered a mild concussion in addition to the bruises and broken bones. And then she realized he was trying to remember her name.

"Maddie. Maddie Montgomery." *I was a year behind you in school. We see each other almost every Sunday at church.*

Well, she saw him anyway. It was pretty clear Aiden hadn't noticed *her*. But then, why would he? They shared the same zip code but were worlds apart when it came to everything else.

"Maddie." There it was. A tiny glimmer of recognition. Very tiny. "I've seen your name on donation receipts for the animal shelter."

While Maddie was trying to decide if she should be amused or offended that her signature was more memorable than her face, Aiden pivoted away from her and shuffled toward the reading nook without a backward glance.

He lowered himself into one of the leather chairs and then proceeded to ignore both the coffee and the magazines.

Okay, then.

Time to get back to work.

Fifteen minutes later, Maddie decided that was easier said than done. Aiden was proving more irresistible to the people who wandered into the library than the pot of freshly brewed pumpkin spice coffee.

Maddie, whose first order of business was straightening the shelves after Mr. Elliott's sixth-graders had invaded the poetry section the day before, would hear the door open and start a countdown in her head. There would be five seconds of silence and then a cheerful, "Aiden! How are you doing?"

To which Aiden would respond with an equally cheerful, "Great."

Maddie wondered if she was the only one who knew he was lying.

If one more person asked Aiden how he was doing, he was going to run screaming from the building.

Except…he couldn't run. At the moment, the only thing he'd be able to manage was a fast limp. Maybe.

But that would also draw the kind of attention Aiden had been hoping to avoid while waiting for his ride to physical therapy. He'd figured the clinic's central pick-up point—the local library—wouldn't exactly be a hotbed of activity this time of day.

He'd figured wrong. Over the past half hour, a steady stream of people had invaded his space, clucking over his injuries, their eyes filled with sympathy.

Aiden hated being the focus of anyone's sympathy. So he'd scraped up a smile, even though the med van driver was twenty minutes late and the thought of another round of PT was making his leg throb more than usual. Not to mention the itch he couldn't scratch without ripping off the cast on his arm first.

Six. Weeks. That's how long he had to wear the stupid

thing. With good behavior, Aiden hoped he could talk the doctor into reducing his sentence to three.

You really caught a break, the surgeon who'd pinned Aiden's wrist back together had told him.

Yeah, well, Aiden didn't feel as if he'd caught a break. He felt, as a matter of fact, broken.

Scratch that. He *was* broken.

He was angry, too, although the anger wasn't visible, like the rest of the cuts and bruises. It wasn't healing as quickly, either.

The telephone began to ring, and the librarian emerged from behind a wall of bookcases. She didn't so much as glance in Aiden's direction as she glided toward the desk, the soles of her ballet-style slippers barely making a sound against the gleaming hardwood floor.

Guilt, not pain, had Aiden shifting in his chair.

He'd gotten into a lot of trouble when he was growing up, but quickly learned there was something about his smile that always got him out of it. That he hadn't been able to instantly produce one of those smiles in the presence of a pretty girl was further proof that some injuries didn't show up on an X-ray.

And the librarian *was* pretty, a detail Aiden hadn't noticed during their first encounter. Acute humiliation could have that effect on a guy. A month ago, he'd beaten his older brothers to the top of Eagle Rock without breaking a sweat, and now a rug, one in the shape of a ladybug, no less, had had the power to throw him off balance.

Aiden gave Maddie Montgomery another covert glance as she picked up the phone.

Champagne-blond hair was bundled into a tidy little knot at the base of Maddie's neck, but the oversize, rectangular glasses perched on her nose didn't detract from a heart-shaped face and porcelain skin. Coupled with a slender frame and diminutive height, the overall effect made her look like a studious woodland pixie.

A studious woodland pixie whom Aiden had been rude to.

The lack of physical activity was making him cranky, and it hadn't helped knowing Maddie must have seen him conk himself in the head with his cast.

Aiden was used to being in control, but now he felt like a marionette with a couple of broken strings. And the fact that a woman whose head barely reached the top of his shoulder had felt the need to come to his rescue when he'd tripped on the rug…well, that made Aiden cranky, too.

"Aiden!"

Aiden stifled a groan as a woman with a helmet of iron-gray curls marched up to him. When he'd chosen the library as a hiding place, he hadn't considered it might be the stomping grounds for retired elementary school teachers.

"Mrs. Hammond." Aiden pushed himself up in the chair and tried not to wince when pain rocketed down his leg and funneled into all five toes. "How are you?"

Mrs. Hammond peered down at him, eyes narrowed. Aiden's former teacher might have lost an inch or two in height over the years, but her power to intimidate hadn't diminished at all.

"It's sweet of you to ask, but I'm not the one with the broken bones, now, am I?" she countered. "How are *you*?"

"Great." A noise that sounded suspiciously like a snort came from the direction of the circulation desk.

Aiden glanced at Maddie, but she had her back to him as she tapped away on her keyboard. It must have been his imagination. Aiden didn't know much about librarians, but he figured she wouldn't deliberately break the number one rule—Quiet, Please—printed on the poster above her desk.

Mrs. Hammond clucked her tongue. "That bump on

your head looks bigger than the one you got when you fell off the top of the slide at recess."

He'd jumped, actually, but Aiden decided not to mention that. Half the population of Castle Falls already thought he was reckless. "It looks worse than it feels."

Way worse. Every time Aiden looked in the mirror, the bruises seemed to have shifted in position and color. There was no getting around it. He was a walking, talking human kaleidoscope.

"I've been out of town, visiting my grandchildren for a few weeks," Mrs. Hammond went on. "I just heard about your accident at choir practice last night."

Accident.

The word boiled inside Aiden. He struggled to clamp down the lid on his emotions, but it didn't stop the memories from rushing back.

He'd been on his way home just after dusk. Window rolled down. Radio cranked up. Tired but exhilarated from a day spent clearing brush for River Quest, an event that Castle Falls Outfitters would be hosting for the first time during the Fall Festival in October.

Aiden's event. His baby.

He'd spent hours plotting the course and planning a variety of land and water challenges guaranteed to stir up some friendly competition. Brendan and Liam, who'd been cautious when Aiden had approached them with the idea, were surprised at the number of teams that had already registered after Lily posted the information to their website.

That was another reason he wanted the event to succeed. The money from the entry fees would bump up the numbers in Castle Falls Outfitters' bank account, proving he was a valuable asset to the family business.

The chance to say "I told you so" was always a bonus, too.

The thought had made Aiden grin. And he'd been grinning when a set of headlights rounded the corner up ahead. In *his* lane…

Aiden had regained consciousness in a sterile hospital room connected to more wires and plastic tubing than a car battery, fire streaking through his veins instead of blood. And his *head*. It had taken every ounce of Aiden's energy to focus on the shadowy silhouettes of the people in the room.

His mother, Sunni, had been sitting in the chair closest to Aiden, head bowed, lips moving in silent prayer. She'd been praying for him for sixteen years, and Aiden doubted that would ever change. His brother Brendan and his wife, Lily, were engaged in quiet conversation at the foot of the bed, and his brother Liam stood near the window, his hands knotted at his sides. The only ones unaccounted for were Anna Leighton, Liam's fiancée, and her eight-year-old daughters, Cassie and Chloe.

An image of the twins' bright smiles had dredged up a wave of fresh pain. What if he wasn't the only one who'd been injured that night?

"Is everybody…okay?"

Aiden's voice—barely more than a croak—had brought everyone to his side in an instant.

"We will be, bro, now that you're awake." Brendan had changed since he'd met the former Lily Michaels, but he still wasn't what you'd call a touchy-feely kind of guy. So the husky rattle in his oldest brother's voice was as unexpected—and unsettling—as the tears glistening in his eyes.

"I meant the people—" Aiden had swallowed and tried again "—in the other car."

Brendan and Liam had exchanged a look.

"Aiden…according to the county deputy, your vehicle was the only one involved," Liam had finally said. "A trucker spotted your pickup in the ditch and called 911.

You were unconscious, so he sat with you until the ambulance arrived."

"The deputy thought the load of lumber in the bed of the truck must have shifted when you rounded the corner," Brendan added. "You tried to overcorrect and ended up in the ditch."

"That's not what happened." Aiden's vehicle had ended up in the ditch because he'd swerved to avoid a head-on collision with the one barreling toward him. "I saw…lights."

Sunni had leaned forward and squeezed his hand. "You have a mild concussion, sweetheart. The doctor warned us that things might be a little fuzzy for a few weeks."

"No—" Aiden had struggled to sit up, but Liam's palm, rimmed with calluses from the hours he spent in the shop, had gently pressed him into the mattress again.

"We can talk about it later. Right now you need to rest."

As if on cue, a nurse had slipped into the room and put something in Aiden's IV that made sure he took his brother's advice.

Over the next forty-eight hours, the fuzziness subsided, but Aiden could still see those lights coming toward him…

"I'm sure Sunni has been worried sick about you."

Aiden blinked and the lights disappeared. Regrettably, Mrs. Hammond was still there, glowering down at him.

"I would think you've caused that poor woman enough sleepless nights."

The meaning was clear. His former teacher, like everyone else in Castle Falls, assumed the accident was Aiden's fault. Because apparently it was easier for people to believe he'd taken the corner too fast than it was to believe someone in their close-knit community had forced him off the road and kept on going.

But the worst part?

Aiden was pretty sure his family believed it, too.

Chapter Two

"You're all set, Mrs. Hammond." Maddie tapped the send key. "The book should be here by the end of the week."

"Thank you so much, Madeline." Beverly Hammond was the only person in Castle Falls who refused to call Maddie by her nickname. The fifth-grade attendance sheet had recorded one Madeline Rose Montgomery, so Madeline she'd remained. "I'll stop by and pick it up first thing Monday morning."

"You've been waiting a year for it to come out, so why don't I bring it to church on Sunday?" Maddie offered.

"That would be wonderful!" Mrs. Hammond leaned closer. "But we have to make a trade. The book for a batch of pecan turtles?"

"Deal!" Her former teacher had a weakness for suspense novels, while Maddie's happened to be chocolate in any shape or form.

It was one of the reasons Maddie had loved growing up in Castle Falls.

People *knew* each other.

Her gaze slid toward the reading nook, something that had been happening way too often over the past half hour.

Judging from the expression on Aiden's face, he wouldn't

put that particular trait on the "pro" column of living in a small town.

Maddie hadn't heard what Mrs. Hammond said to him, but whatever it was had stripped the smile from Aiden's face the moment the woman had walked away. He'd picked up one of the magazines, but Maddie suspected it was a barrier meant to hold people at bay rather than a way to pass the time.

The cell phone in her pocket vibrated, a reminder that the historical society's monthly meeting was scheduled to start in ten minutes.

Encouraging members of the community to see the library as a gathering place had been at the top of Maddie's goals when she'd moved into a full-time position. She'd extended the evening hours two days a week, talked local clubs into holding their meetings in the conference room and hosted special events on the weekends.

Change had taken place slowly—another characteristic of small-town life—but Maddie persevered. Things began to turn around when she showed the mayor's wife how to unlock the secrets of social media. The woman had told a friend…who'd told a friend…who'd told a friend…and suddenly Maddie found herself teaching classes on everything from résumé writing to basic web design. For the last two years, at the request of the high school principal, Maddie had even helped some members of the graduating class with the research for their senior projects.

Her parents had expressed concern over how much time and energy she poured into her job, but Maddie loved every minute of it. And since there was very little chance she'd be blessed with a family of her own someday, Maddie had decided to bloom in the place God had planted her, and nurture the people He brought through the doors of the library instead.

A flash of light outside the window caught Maddie's attention as she stood up from her desk. A white van sporting the logo of a regional medical clinic was rolling up to the curb. A few seconds later, a stocky man vaulted from the driver's seat. The back door slid open and a hydraulic ramp made a slow descent toward the sidewalk. The interior of the van was empty, and the driver looked around.

That's when Maddie realized the van wasn't there to drop someone off. It was there to pick someone *up.*

And she was pretty sure she knew who that someone was. Maddie glanced at the reading nook again. Three members of the historical society had commandeered the table closest to Aiden so they could chat before their meeting started, and two of Maddie's "regulars" stood by the coffeepot, absorbed in conversation.

Aiden continued to stare at the magazine, completely unaware the driver of the medical van was waiting outside. Considering the way he'd reacted when Maddie tried to help him before, she couldn't imagine he would want an audience—or assistance—getting into the van.

Maddie saw the driver look at his watch and figured she had about sixty seconds before he came in.

Without considering all the possible ramifications of her actions—and Maddie *always* considered the possible ramifications of her actions—she walked over to the members of the historical society and eased into their conversation with a smile.

"Good morning, ladies!" She was careful not to look at Aiden. "I reserved the media room until eleven o'clock so you won't have to share the computers with anyone this morning."

Janette Morrison, the society's secretary, patted Maddie on the shoulder. "Thank you again for helping me, Maddie. I couldn't have found Adelle without your detective work."

"You're welcome." Maddie tried not to smile.

While helping the woman trace her family genealogy,

Maddie had discovered a little-known connection to the mysterious Adelle Lewis, the daughter of the wealthy lumber baron who'd founded Castle Falls.

Adelle's name had abruptly disappeared from the society pages and everyone assumed she'd died, but Maddie had traced the young woman's life through a series of old journals and found out that Adelle's parents had disowned her after she'd married a young circuit preacher against their wishes.

Now the historical society viewed Maddie as a sort of twenty-first-century Nancy Drew, able to track down clues in cyberspace, link by link.

"I do have a question about how to use the microfilm scanner," Janette said. "If you can spare a few minutes."

"Of course. I'll grab a cup of coffee and meet you there in a few minutes," Maddie promised, not mentioning the coffee wasn't for her.

Janette looked relieved as the rest of the committee members scooped up their belongings and filed toward the computer room in the back of the library.

"It's pretty chilly out there this morning," Maddie mused out loud. "I thought the med van driver might appreciate a cup of coffee." She filled a disposable cup and turned toward the door.

She could practically feel Aiden's eyes follow her. But would *he*?

The driver waved at Maddie, and she hoped he was a flavored-coffee kind of guy. A group of men who met at the library once a month to play chess claimed that it smelled like potpourri and wouldn't touch the stuff.

"Good morning!" Maddie raised the steaming cup. "We've got curbside delivery today. Pumpkin spice."

"Mmm." The skeptical look on the driver's face belied the teasing sparkle in his eyes. "Does it pair well with a jelly doughnut?"

"In my experience, everything goes with jelly doughnuts." Maddie grinned and handed him the coffee.

She heard the soft click of the door and dared a glance over her shoulder. Aiden had bypassed the handicap-accessible ramp—no surprise there—and was making his way slowly down the concrete steps.

One. Two. Three.

Maddie silently cheered Aiden on until he reached the sidewalk. And lurched past her without a word. Again.

The driver tossed back a swallow of coffee and looked Aiden over. "PT?"

"Yup." Aiden bared his teeth in a smile. "That's me."

Maddie turned away, knowing it was the driver's job to assist his passenger even if said passenger didn't want—or appreciate—the assistance.

But at least she'd made sure that Aiden no longer had an audience.

"Thanks, Pixie."

It took a moment for Maddie to realize Aiden was talking to her. But he had to be, considering the only other person within earshot happened to be the burly guy climbing into the driver's seat of the van.

But… Pixie? Seriously? He'd already forgotten her name?

"It's *Maddie*—"

Aiden's smile—this time a genuine, no-holds-barred, steal-the-breath-from-a-girl's-lungs smile—was the last thing Maddie saw before the door slid shut.

Making her wonder if he'd forgotten at all.

Aiden's hand tightened on the handle of the crutch as he stared out the window of the sunroom.

Autumn was his favorite time of year. Crimson trees lined both sides of the bank like torches, the sapphire-blue river the base of the flames. For Aiden, it was like paddling through a fiery corridor. Even on sunny days, the breeze carried a bite that stirred his senses. Made him feel alive.

Rich Mason, Sunni's husband and Aiden's foster dad, had teased Aiden about having river water flowing through his veins instead of blood. But for a ten-year-old boy who'd grown up surrounded by concrete, the river had proved more fascinating than a playground.

On the water, Aiden could move at his own pace. There was no one telling him to take it easy, slow down or—his least favorite of the three—stop.

And now, sixteen years later, over the course of a day, he'd heard every single one.

Aiden's simmering frustration had turned into a rolling boil when he got home from therapy and saw the envelope on the coffee table. A few days after he'd been released from the hospital, Aiden had called the sheriff's department and requested a copy of the deputy's report from the night he'd been injured.

Aiden had practically ripped the document in his haste to open it. He skimmed through it, hoping to see something—*anything*—that would support his claim that another vehicle had been involved.

No skid marks, the officer had noted on the bottom.

Aiden had wanted to throw back his head and howl. There weren't any skid marks because the vehicle in the oncoming lane hadn't braked. And Aiden hadn't had time to, either. If he'd been a minute earlier or a minute later, things would have turned out differently.

Why hadn't God intervened on Aiden's behalf?

That question had continued to plague him since the night of the accident, slowly chiseling away at the foundation of what he'd thought was an unshakeable faith with the cold, relentless pull of an undertow.

Aiden tried to shore it up by reciting scripture he'd memorized and pulling up the lyrics from praise songs, but over the past few days, the doubts had slowly claimed more territory.

But his family worried enough about his injuries. Aiden wasn't about to admit his trust in God had sustained damage in the accident, too.

The door swung open and Aiden pressed out a smile for his brothers as they strode into the room.

"Missing something?" Brendan held up Aiden's cell phone. "I found this on the bench in the laundry room."

That's because Aiden had left it there. An abandoned cell phone equaled freedom from emails, text messages and happy-face emojis.

"Oops." Aiden pointed at his head. "Concussion."

He'd been kidding, but instead of making a smart comeback, guilt flashed in his oldest brother's eyes.

"Sorry," Brendan murmured.

So was Aiden. Sorry his brothers felt the need to tiptoe around him when they used to wrestle him to the ground. Sorry they had to shoulder Aiden's share of the work around the place in addition to their own, while squeezing in time to complete the course for River Quest.

Liam's plan to finish the cabin that he and Anna and the twins would call home after the couple exchanged their wedding vows on Christmas Eve had been delayed because of Aiden, too.

With a damaged knee, climbing the thirteen steps up to the garage apartment he shared with Liam would have been as impossible as scaling a mountain. And because all the bedrooms in Sunni's house were upstairs, too, Liam, the brother with the mad design skills, had been charged with converting the sunroom overlooking the river into a bedroom before Aiden was released from the hospital.

His family assumed that seeing the river outside his window would comfort him. But like a kid with his nose pressed against the glass of the candy store window, all it did was give Aiden a perfect view of everything he couldn't have.

"How did therapy go today?" Liam asked.

Teeth-gritting, stomach-turning, excruciatingly painful. "Great."

"Great," Liam echoed, relief chasing the concern from his eyes.

How was it that Aiden could fool his brothers—the brothers who'd lived with him for twenty-six years—and a petite librarian with fern green eyes had seen right through him? Recognized him for the faker that he was?

Aiden didn't have time to dwell on that—or why he *remembered* the color of Maddie Montgomery's eyes—because Liam was nodding at Brendan, and Brendan… cleared his throat.

Aiden's internal alarm system instantly went on high alert. If his oldest brother was struggling to find the right thing to say, chances were good it would be something Aiden didn't want to hear.

"Don't tell me this is another family meeting." As far as Aiden was concerned, the last one hadn't gone so well.

He was still trying to wrap his head around the fact that their biological mother had kept her fourth pregnancy a secret and given a baby girl—Aiden's baby sister—up for adoption after she was born.

And as much as Aiden loved and respected his oldest brother, he wasn't thrilled Brendan had kept that a secret until a few months ago.

"Not tod—" Brendan caught himself. "Of course not. Liam and I need your opinion about something."

Since when?

Aiden clamped down on the words so hard that pain shot down his jaw.

But he knew what Brendan and Liam were trying to do. It was the same thing everyone—from Sunni to Anna's eight-year-old twins—had been trying to do since the day Aiden was released from the hospital. They wanted him to feel useful.

But what his family didn't seem to understand was the more they tried to make Aiden feel useful, the more useless he felt.

It was bad enough he'd been as helpless as a baby those first few days at home. Liam had had to help Aiden shower and get dressed. Brendan—Mr. Organized—had bought one of those plastic pill holders and divvied up Aiden's pain meds in compartments that corresponded with the days of the week. His brothers had even taken turns checking on Aiden after he went to bed until he'd asked for a story, too.

They'd taken the hint and backed off. Now Aiden realized he'd simply been granted a temporary reprieve from "brother smother" while they plotted a new strategy.

"I printed out the map you drew." A map Liam happened to have tucked in the back pocket of his jeans. "Do you have time to take a look at it?"

"Sure." The word tasted bitter in Aiden's mouth. Thanks to the guy who'd run him off the road, he had nothing *but* time.

He'd imagined being involved in every aspect of River Quest, and now he'd been reduced to the role of consultant. It was killing Aiden to watch his idea take shape under someone else's hands—even if those hands belonged to his more-than-capable older brothers.

"The fire ring—" Liam pushed aside the flotsam and jetsam that had collected on the coffee table over the course of the day and set the map down. "It looks a little close to the victory platform."

"It's not a fire ring…it's a ring of fire."

Brendan frowned. "What's the difference?"

Aiden couldn't believe he had to ask. "One you roast marshmallows over, and one you run through."

"Run through," Liam repeated.

"Is there an echo in here?" Aiden rolled his eyes toward the knotty pine ceiling. "What did you think? We'd be making s'mores for all the contestants when they got to the end of the race?"

Judging from their expressions, that was exactly what his brothers had thought.

"You expect people to run through fire," Brendan said slowly. "On purpose."

"If they want to win. Hence the word *challenge*."

A smile played at the corners of Liam's lips. "It will definitely be that."

"It will also send our liability insurance premiums through the roof," Brendan muttered.

"Everyone has to sign a waiver," Aiden reminded him.

"Fine...but that doesn't mean s'mores are a bad idea."

Aiden hadn't expected Brendan to go along with it. Did his big brother trust his judgment? Or did this fall under "humoring the patient"?

There was no way to know for sure until Aiden could sneak the side-by-side out of the garage when no one was looking and take a drive back into the woods himself.

Being under constant surveillance had joined the list of things that made Aiden feel twitchy. And speaking of constant surveillance...

"Where's Mom? She mentioned something about going out for dinner tonight." Aiden didn't look forward to being on display for the whole town to see, but sitting at the table, underneath the family microscope, was taking its toll on him, too.

"She is, but not with you." Liam got a goofy, lovesick grin on his face. "She and Lily are meeting Anna at The Happy Cow tonight to work on the wedding plans."

Aiden tried to hide his relief. He'd be alone.

"So we ordered a pizza."

Or not.

"Sausage with extra mushroom," Brendan added.

Aiden's favorite. "Humoring the patient" it was.

"Sounds great. I'll meet you in the family room." At least there wasn't a wall of glass framing the river, reminding Aiden that he could look but not touch.

Liam shook his head.

"You stay put. We'll bring it here."

Aiden kept the smile in place until his brothers left the room, and waited until their voices faded before he took out everything on the coffee table—including the map—with one swipe of his crutch.

Because the reminder that Liam and Anna would be exchanging their vows in a few short months reminded Aiden of a vow *he'd* made. He'd stood in this very room a few weeks ago and announced to his entire family that he would track down their missing sister before the wedding.

What had he been thinking?

Right now, the task seemed as impossible as sprinting through the ring of fire Aiden had designed for River Quest.

Hiring a private investigator wasn't in the budget, and the thought of spending hours on the computer made Aiden feel twitchy all over again. He'd never understood why people would rather stare at a screen than the sky, anyway. A person should experience life, not read about it.

Aiden bent down to collect the items on the floor before his brothers returned, and he picked up the book Chloe had been reading during her "entertain Aiden" shift the day before.

A bookmark, stamped with gold and copper leaves, poked out between the pages.

Fall into a Good Book. Visit Your Local Library.

Aiden's lips twisted in a smile.

Maybe he didn't know where to start the search for their missing sister...but he knew someone who might.

Chapter Three

For over an hour on Friday evening, Maddie had been pounding her head against the proverbial brick wall, trying to coax even a spark of interest from the three high school seniors who'd gathered around the table in the library's conference room.

A feat Aiden Kane accomplished simply by walking through the door.

Tyler Olsen slipped his cell phone back into the pocket of his hoodie, and Justin Wagner, whose chin had been fused to his chest from the moment he'd sat down, pushed upright in his chair. Skye Robinson, who'd been doodling on the cover of her notebook during Maddie's opening introduction, took one look at Aiden and her cheeks turned the same shade of bubble-gum pink as her lip gloss.

Not that Maddie could blame her.

The guy took faded denim and flannel to a whole new level.

The patch that had covered Aiden's eye was gone, and Maddie felt the full impact of his cobalt-blue gaze. Her heart began to perform a series of crazy little pirouettes inside her chest that might have, under different circumstances, warranted a call to the heart specialist Maddie saw once a year.

"The sign in the window said Closed, but the door was unlocked…" A casual shrug punctuated the statement, hinting that Aiden was the kind of man who viewed posted hours as a guideline, not a hard-and-fast rule. "Sorry for interrupting."

Maddie hadn't bothered to lock the front door because Castle Falls rolled up its streets after six o'clock this time of year. And the only thing Aiden had interrupted was the silence that had been hanging over the room like a blanket of fog since the teenagers had arrived.

It was the second time that week Maddie had met with the three students, but she'd never met a group so resistant to her help. Maddie had a hunch it was because these particular seniors, unlike the others she'd worked with in the past, hadn't *asked* for it.

When the principal had called and given her the names of the teenagers she'd be working with, he'd asked Maddie to have them sign an attendance sheet. Maddie naively assumed it was a new policy, until they'd slinked through the door.

One look at the expressions on their faces, and Maddie knew they didn't see the library as the starting point that would set them on an exciting course to their futures. No, in their minds it equaled two hours of detention, and Maddie was their warden.

The icebreaker she had chosen for the opening session on Monday night had been a complete failure, and they didn't seem particularly interested in this evening's presentation about the importance of research, either.

As a matter of fact, the three teenagers didn't seem to be interested in *anything.*

Until Aiden crashed the study session.

Maddie had no idea why he was here, but she closed her laptop. "You're not interrupting. We're almost finished."

A collective sigh of relief traveled around the table and Maddie tried not to take it personally.

"Great." Aiden smiled his quicksilver smile. "Do you mind if I hang around for a few minutes?"

Fortunately, he didn't wait for her answer.

Because the musky scent of autumn leaves and fresh balsam clinging to Aiden's jacket as he claimed an empty chair was overriding the "walk in the woods" diffuser on the mantel—and apparently Maddie's ability to put together a coherent sentence, as well.

Focus on your notes, Maddie.

She put a checkmark next to The Importance of Research. "On Monday, I'd like everyone to bring a list of possible topics, and we'll try to narrow it down to your top two."

"Why can't you just tell us what to do?" Tyler asked.

"The faculty wants your senior presentation to be more personal than a term paper or essay," Maddie said. "They're not only interested in what you've learned over the past four years, they're interested in *you*."

"Yeah, right," Skye muttered.

Maddie knew better than to engage in something that could potentially turn into a debate. "If you're having trouble finding a topic, I've encouraged other students to look at the results of their career assessment surveys for ideas."

Her suggestion was met with blank stares.

"You haven't taken it yet?" Maddie asked cautiously.

"What's a career assessment survey?" Skye wanted to know.

Well, that answered her question.

"It's a series of questions that helps you determine what career might fit you best."

Skye's eyes narrowed. "Sounds like a test."

"Actually, it can be kind of fun," Maddie said. "The questions are designed to help you pinpoint your interests, discover your gifts and abilities. And the results can help you decide what degree you'll pursue in college."

"College?" Tyler scoffed. "I'm not even sure I'm going to graduate from high school."

Maddie made a mental note to call the guidance office first thing on Monday morning and find out more about the students she'd volunteered to help.

"Okay." She exhaled a silent prayer for wisdom. "If you can't find time to take it at school, I'll see if you can take the test online at the library during our next session. Trust me—it will make choosing a topic for your presentation much easier."

The word *presentation* elicited another group sigh.

Maddie stifled one of her own. Unless the principal had made attendance for the study sessions mandatory, there was no guarantee she'd ever see them again.

"I think that's it for tonight." Maddie waited for the inevitable stampede out the door, but suddenly the teenagers who'd fidgeted through her entire PowerPoint no longer seemed to be in a hurry to leave.

Justin drifted over to the plate of chocolate chip cookies Maddie had set out before the meeting, and Skye began to apply another layer of lip gloss. Tyler, who hadn't paid any attention to the folder Maddie had given him, took his time sliding it into his empty backpack. When he finally got it positioned just right, his eyes locked on Aiden.

"I saw your picture in the paper."

"Yeah?" Aiden stiffened, but Tyler didn't seem to notice.

"Yeah. That rope bridge you're building over the river… it sounds pretty sweet, man."

The confused look on Aiden's face told Maddie he hadn't seen the most recent issue of the local newspaper. She retrieved the copy draped over the wire rack in the corner and set it down in front of him.

"It's an article highlighting the activities for the fall festival." Maddie had read it, too. Castle Falls Outfitters would be hosting a new event called River Quest during the weekend-long celebration, and the reporter had interviewed Aiden because he was the one who'd come up with the idea.

Some of the challenges sounded downright dangerous to Maddie, but she supposed that was part of their appeal. Until now, the most risky event in town had been the Five Alarm Chili Cook-Off.

Aiden's gaze dropped to the black-and-white photograph on the front page. It had obviously been taken before the accident. He was leaning against the Castle Falls Outfitters sign, wearing jeans, a T-shirt with the Castle Falls logo on the front, and his signature grin.

"The headline is clever," Maddie said, then read it out loud. *"River Quest Promises Thrills, Chills and Possible Spills."*

Aiden might have agreed—if a knot the size of a baseball wasn't clogging his throat.

He remembered the day the reporter had called and asked if he would be available for an interview.

"Let me check my calendar," Aiden had joked. What he'd really needed was time to absorb the fact that the reporter wanted to meet with *him* instead of Brendan or Liam.

Aiden's name was listed on the home page of the Castle Falls Outfitters website, but unlike his brothers, it wasn't as if he'd accomplished something significant enough to *earn* his spot there.

River Quest was supposed to have changed that.

The interview had taken place a few weeks ago, and Aiden assumed the reporter had scrapped the whole thing after the accident, but here he was. On the front page. And apparently it didn't matter that some of the details were no longer accurate.

Aiden had told the reporter that he planned to test the entire course himself before the fall festival, and now he'd be watching from the sidelines as a spectator.

On top of the world one day. Trapped underneath his pickup truck the next.

I don't get it, God...

"Is there really a cave behind the waterfall on your property?" The girl with the lavender stripes in her hair pressed closer for a better look.

The fragrance she was wearing made Aiden's nose sting, but he jerked his chin in a nod. "The cave is the starting point for the competition. Each team has to go through the tunnel and retrieve their flag. The one with the best time gets to skip the next challenge."

The kid sitting next to Aiden shrugged. "That doesn't sound very tough."

Aiden found himself staring into the restless, prove-it-to-me eyes of his younger self. "It's not. Just really, really dark."

"No flashlight?"

"No light at all," Aiden said. "Just you and a space about two feet wide."

The buzz of the kid's cell phone extinguished the flicker of interest in his eyes. He was on his feet before he'd even finished reading the incoming text and, without a word to Maddie or his friends, bolted for the door.

The other two exchanged a look, snatched up their backpacks and followed.

"If you have any questions before our next meeting," Maddie called after them, "don't hesitate to email me or stop—"

The door snapped shut.

"I don't know about you, but I'm pretty sure I won them

over." A dimple that had been hiding in Maddie's cheek came out to play. "Are you waiting for someone again? Or did you want to check out a book?"

Aiden was still distracted by that intriguing dimple, and it took a moment for the words to sink in.

"I don't read."

"You don't..." Maddie stopped. Cleared her throat. "Then why—"

"I came to see you." Aiden suddenly realized that hadn't come out quite the way he'd intended it when Maddie's big green eyes got even bigger. "One of the women who was here on Monday morning...she said you'd helped her find someone named Adelle."

"Janette Morrison." Maddie tipped her head, and a strand of pale blond hair slipped free from the bun at the base of her neck. "You're interested in tracing your family genealogy, too?"

His family genealogy?

"Never mind." Aiden planted his crutch against the floor and levered himself out of the chair. "It was stupid..."

And so was he. For eavesdropping on a conversation. For totally misunderstanding said conversation.

For thinking this was a good idea.

He made it two steps before Maddie landed in front of him, cutting off his escape.

"Aiden...wait."

Even with a broken wrist and two cracked ribs, Aiden could have brushed Maddie Montgomery aside with no more effort than it would have taken to shoo away a butterfly. But because Sunni insisted her sons use good manners, he produced a grin instead.

"Look, no worries. I'm sorry for barging in on your study session tonight." Aiden tried to ease around her and found his path blocked again.

"Who do you want to find?"

Aiden opened his mouth to tell Maddie that he didn't want her help after all, but what came out instead was, "My sister."

"I… I didn't know you had a sister."

"I didn't either, until a few months ago." Aiden couldn't prevent the bitterness from seeping into his voice.

But Maddie didn't gasp or pelt him with questions. She waited, her silence giving Aiden the freedom to retreat or explain.

Retreat seemed like the better option. Until now, it hadn't occurred to Aiden that asking for help would mean opening the door to the past and allowing someone to see the skeletons rattling around in the Kane family closet.

He and his brothers had moved to Castle Falls when they were kids, but the past cast a long shadow. People still didn't understand why the Masons had become foster parents and opened their home—and their hearts—to three troubled boys. And when Rich had unexpectedly passed away from a heart attack six months later, some of Sunni's closest friends had encouraged her to send Aiden and his brothers back to Detroit.

Sunni had listened to God and adopted them instead, although they hadn't legally changed their last name to Mason. Aiden hadn't questioned the reasons behind that decision—or who'd made it—until Brendan had finally gotten around to telling the rest of the family they had a sister out there who might want to find them someday.

And family meant everything to Aiden.

He hadn't been wanted—something Carla Kane had reminded Aiden often enough—but it was tearing him apart inside that their younger sister might have grown up believing the same thing.

"Our biological mother gave the baby up for adoption after she was born," he finally said. "I thought…"

"I might know how to find her," Maddie finished.

"Right." Aiden touched the bandage on his forehead, hoping Maddie would dismiss the crazy notion as a side effect of his injuries. Playing the concussion card had worked pretty well with his brothers, after all.

"Maddie?"

They both turned toward the doorway, and Maddie's face lit with a smile.

"Dad! I didn't expect to see you until tomorrow night."

A man with thinning gray hair and a frame the width of Aiden's fly rod stepped into the room.

"I didn't mean to intrude." His gaze bounced from Maddie to Aiden and then back again. "I found some of those apples you like at the grocery store and thought I'd drop them off on my way home."

"That wouldn't be because you're hoping I have time to make a pie for dessert tomorrow night, now, would it?" Maddie teased.

"Of course not." Her dad flicked a look at Aiden. "I know how precious your free time is, sweetheart."

Aiden didn't miss the subtle implication that there were people in the room who didn't.

"The door to my apartment is open." Maddie's smile didn't waver. "I'll meet you upstairs in a few minutes. Aiden just had a question for me."

The only thing that moved was the man's eyebrows. They sank together over the bridge of his nose in a frown that had probably scared away every guy who'd dared to ask Maddie out on a date.

It was a good thing Aiden didn't scare easily.

Whoa. Where had *that* thought come from?

Not that Aiden had a problem asking a girl out. But like his brother Liam had so helpfully pointed out a few months ago, Aiden's problem was that he never followed up with a second or third date.

Because of that, he'd gotten a reputation for avoiding

commitment when the opposite was true. Because of his childhood, Aiden understood its value more than most guys his age. He never made promises he didn't intend to keep. Aiden wasn't a heartbreaker, but until he met a woman he could trust—with the good, the bad *and* the ugly—he stuck to the shallow end of the dating pool.

"That's okay." He tucked the crutch under his arm. "I have to go, anyway." Sunni, who'd dropped Aiden off while she ran a few errands in town, was probably wondering where he was.

He took a step forward, but this time, instead of stopping him, Maddie escorted him past her father and into the narrow hallway outside the conference room.

"You don't have to walk me to the door, you know." Aiden's lips twisted in a wry smile. "I'll watch for rugs this time."

Maddie tilted her head back to look up at him, and Aiden waited in vain for the dimple to appear.

Nope. Not happening. Once again, Aiden got the feeling she could see right through him.

"The library closes at two o'clock tomorrow," she said. "But I'll be working a few extra hours, going through donations for the used book sale."

Her meaning was clear—if he wanted to continue their conversation. But Aiden didn't respond.

Because right now, as anxious as he was to find his sister, Aiden wasn't sure Maddie Montgomery and her fern green eyes wouldn't prove more of a hindrance than a help. Because, oh man, he was distracted around her.

Chapter Four

Maddie started the countdown as her dad followed her up the staircase to the second floor.

Five. Four. Three. Two…

"I don't like the idea of strangers wandering in off the street when you're alone in the library at night, sweetheart," he said.

Maddie tamped down a smile. When it came to her dad, the saying about old habits being hard to break had proved true. William and Tara Montgomery had loved and protected Maddie for twenty-five years. She'd been out on her own for several years now, but her dad never failed to come up with a reason to stop by and "check on things." What he was really checking on was her.

"Aiden isn't exactly a stranger, Dad," she reminded him. "You see him every Sunday morning at church."

"I see him staring out the window while Pastor Seth gives the message," her dad grumbled. "He might be sitting in the chair, but it's obvious his mind is somewhere else."

Maddie wasn't about to admit she'd noticed that, too. Because it would mean admitting that she'd noticed Aiden Kane.

You and every other unattached female in town, she chided herself.

"I left the door unlocked in case another student showed up for the study session, and Aiden saw the lights on," Maddie told him. "He didn't realize the library was closed for the evening."

Her dad reached the door at the top of the stairs before Maddie, and it swung open at the touch of his hand. "You should keep this one locked, too."

"No one can access my apartment from the street," Maddie reminded him.

When the title of head librarian had transferred to her after Mrs. Whitman's retirement, Maddie had been given the keys to the studio apartment on the second floor of the building, too.

The space was small, but Maddie loved every inch of it. She'd sewn slipcovers for the sofa and decorated the interior with an eclectic style she liked to call thrift shop chic. A folding screen separated the kitchen from the living room, and African violets bloomed in the window. An old steamer trunk served double duty as a coffee table and storage for the surplus of books when the shelves began to overflow.

Growing up, the characters in the books Maddie read had become her closest friends, so she hadn't been able to part with a single one. For Maddie, sharing a favorite book was like sharing a secret. You weren't just giving people a book. You were offering them a glimpse into your heart.

I don't read.

Maddie was still having a hard time processing what Aiden had said. Not only the words themselves, but the matter-of-fact tone in which they'd been delivered. The way someone might say, "I don't eat kale."

"Maddie?"

Oops. "Sorry, Dad. What did you say?"

"I just want you to be careful, that's all."

"I am careful. And I'll lock the door from now on," Maddie promised.

"I wasn't talking about the door." Her dad hesitated. "I was talking about Aiden Kane. From what I've heard, he can be impulsive and a little reckless. Not the type of man who's looking to settle down."

"*Settle*—" Maddie almost choked on the word. "Aiden isn't interested in going out with me, Dad."

Even if she couldn't deny that for a moment—a teeny tiny moment—her heart had performed that crazy tap dance again when he'd said, "I came to see you."

A response as ridiculous as Aiden asking her out on a date. They had nothing in common. Whenever New Life Fellowship sponsored a hiking trip or a weekend of downhill skiing, Aiden would be listed as the contact person in the church newsletter. Maddie knew that information before anyone else in the congregation because she was the one who typed the monthly newsletter.

She also knew the first four or five names on the sign-up sheet would inevitably be grown-up versions of the athletic, outdoorsy type of girls Aiden had dated in high school.

Maddie hadn't dated in high school. Guys never asked her to go out for a movie and burger. They'd asked her for her help with English homework instead.

"I think that sigh—" her dad pressed a kiss against the top of Maddie's head "—is my cue to leave."

"Sorry, Dad. I've got a lot on my mind tonight, I guess."

He gave her a look. "That wouldn't be because you have too much on your plate, now, would it?"

"I like being busy." Maddie linked arms with him as they walked to the door. "But if you want me to cut something out of my schedule, I don't have to make dessert for Saturday night," she teased.

"Never mind." Her dad's eyes went wide with mock horror. "I take it back!"

The weekly dinners had become a tradition, Maddie's way of showing her parents she hadn't abandoned them, she'd simply moved into her own place like a lot of other people her age. They always spent the evening catching up on each other's lives, and then her dad would break out Scrabble or the cribbage board.

Yet another reason Maddie wasn't Aiden Kane's type.

"I thought you'd say that." Maddie hugged her dad goodbye and closed the door before another sigh slipped out.

Contrary to what her dad feared, Aiden didn't want to date her. He needed her help finding his sister.

Maddie flopped into a chair and curled her feet underneath her, questions multiplying like the maple leaves underneath the tree outside the window.

Did Aiden regret telling her? Did his abrupt departure mean he was going to give up the search before he'd even begun?

Maddie wouldn't. She would have gladly given up half her bedroom—and space on her bookshelves—for a sister or brother. But her parents had found love later in life, and Maddie's traumatic birth and the two heart surgeries that followed had dictated she remain an only child. It had also significantly reduced the chances of her ever having a child of her own.

She knew that God had richly blessed her in other ways—a job she loved, a purpose and a passion—so the pain of knowing she'd never be a mother had eventually subsided. But there were times—like right now—when Maddie felt the ache all over again, a weight pressing down on the sensitive scar tissue of an old wound.

She'd never told anyone her secret. It was her burden to carry. And the truth was, there'd never been a need. The boys who hadn't noticed her in school had grown into men who'd fallen in love and married her pretty, more outgoing classmates. Maddie had been the quiet girl in the library.

Her lips tipped in a smile.

She was *still* the quiet girl in the library. And although Maddie liked and accepted that girl a lot more than she had in high school, it stirred up all kinds of dreams she had no business dreaming. Especially about Aiden Kane.

Maybe there was a woman out there who would eventually change his mind about settling down.

But Maddie knew it wouldn't be her.

Lights illuminated the row of windows on the second floor as Aiden let himself out of the library. A gray Subaru idled at the curb, and before Aiden could take another step, Sunni had hopped out from the driver's seat and jogged around the front of the vehicle to open his door.

Needing a chauffeur was another humbling side effect of Aiden's injuries. It ranked right up there with knowing he'd lose to his mom in a footrace.

"I hope I'm not late. I ran into Rebecca at the grocery store and we chatted for a few minutes."

Aiden didn't have to ask what—or rather *whom*—the topic of conversation had been. Rebecca Tamblin was Pastor Seth's wife and the head of New Life Fellowship's prayer chain. Aiden's name had been at the top of the list for almost two weeks.

"Not a problem." Aiden squeezed out a smile as he folded himself into the passenger seat.

Sunni waited until he buckled up before she steered the car back onto the street.

"Are you too tired to take a little detour on the way home? Dr. Voss called me a few minutes ago and asked if we have room at the shelter for another dog."

Aiden had passed tired a few hours ago and was skidding toward exhausted, but he nodded. "Go for it."

His mom took her responsibilities as the recently appointed chairman of the animal shelter as seriously as she did the family business.

"I was hoping you'd say that!" Sunni flashed a smile and turned left off Riverside, Castle Falls' main street. "Did you find what you were looking for at the library?"

An image of Maddie Montgomery's face danced in Aiden's mind, and he batted it away.

"No." Aiden wasn't ready to confide in his mom yet. If the search for his sister ended in a crash and burn, he wanted to spare his family a ringside seat. Not only that, given Sunni's growing reputation as a matchmaker, Aiden ran the risk she might read something more into his decision to ask a certain librarian for help.

"Wasn't Maddie there?"

"You know her?" As soon as the words slipped out, Aiden realized how ridiculous they sounded. Unlike Aiden, Sunni had lived in Castle Falls most of her life. She probably knew Maddie's favorite color and her birthday.

"I know you didn't graduate together, but she's at church every Sunday." Sunni slid a sideways glance in Aiden's direction. "I'm surprised your paths haven't crossed."

Aiden wasn't. Not after he'd seen Maddie flinch when he said he didn't read. What he should have said was that he didn't read *well*. Reading usually involved sitting still, and sitting still had never come easily to Aiden, either.

He'd rather stick to the things he was good at.

"How is the plan for the new addition coming along?" Aiden steered the conversation to safer ground.

"Wonderful. Between the silent auction last June and a generous donation from the bank a few weeks ago, we should be able to break ground in May.

"The committee decided that since the last meet and

greet for the shelter went over so well, we're going to host another one during the Fall Festival." Sunni chuckled. "Of course, Cassie and Chloe voted that we set up the tent in the backyard."

The gathering point for River Quest. Aiden was glad the darkness cloaked his expression. He gritted his teeth behind a smile. "Good idea."

Everyone was full of good ideas these days. Orders for Liam's new line of vintage canoes had picked up after Lily, the family marketing whiz, had posted a photograph of one on the home page of the website. Anna had taken charge of the Trading Post, and the twins helped on the weekends, straightening shelves and greeting customers.

Everyone, it seemed, had something valuable to offer. Everyone except Aiden.

Although he should have been used to that by now.

Lights glowed in the windows of the veterinary clinic, but Sunni cruised past the front entrance and drove around to the back of the building.

The door swung open before Aiden had a chance to knock, and Dr. Voss motioned them inside.

"Sunni. Aiden. Come in, come in." The veterinarian's eyes were bloodshot, and the tufts of reddish-brown hair that sprouted from his head now lay as flat as stalks of wheat after a killing frost. "It's been a long day. Two emergency surgeries, which is the reason I called you. I'm afraid there's no more room at the inn."

"That's why we're here." Sunni gave the man's arm a comforting squeeze. "I'm glad the shelter could help."

"Follow me." The tails of the veterinarian's wrinkled lab coat flapped against his legs as he led them down the hallway.

It wasn't the first time Aiden had been to the clinic—he'd transported at least a dozen critters there for vaccinations since the shelter's official grand opening—so he expected Dr. Voss to usher them into the spacious room that housed the kennels. The veterinarian walked past the door and took a sharp turn down another, shorter hallway instead.

"Is the dog in quarantine or something?" Aiden whispered to his mom even though he knew it didn't matter. Sunni had a soft spot for hard-luck cases.

If Aiden was ever in danger of forgetting that, all he had to do was look in the mirror.

"Not in quarantine." Dr. Voss was the one who answered the question. "He's kind of a loner…being around the other dogs seems to agitate him. Our facility isn't set up for long-term convalescence, so that's why I called your mother."

"Why isn't it going home?" Aiden asked.

"He doesn't have one at the moment," Sunni said.

Dr. Voss's steps slowed, and he matched his pace to Aiden's. "A hiker found the dog caught in a trap by the river and called the sheriff's department. When Deputy Bristow brought it in, the animal was dehydrated and hypothermic. Its leg wasn't broken, but infection from the wound had spread, so we had to get that under control. What he needs now is rest and a little TLC."

Aiden figured the "TLC" part was where his mom came in.

"What about its owner? Don't you think someone is looking for him?"

A look passed between Dr. Voss and his mom, a hint they'd had this conversation before.

"I highly doubt it," the vet finally said. "The X-rays I took show…older…injuries. The deputy found evidence the owner was hunting out of season, so if he does step up to claim the dog, he'd be facing questions he won't want to answer."

So rather than get into trouble, the owner had simply abandoned the animal.

Dr. Voss stopped in front of a door and slipped his hand inside to flip the light on. A row of large wire crates—all empty except the one filled with rags—lined the wall.

"Where—" Aiden's throat convulsed, sealing off the rest of the sentence, when the bundle of rags moved. Took on the shape of a dog.

His mom's gasp of dismay broke the silence, and the veterinarian's lips flattened in agreement.

"Believe it or not, he actually looks better than he did when the deputy brought him in. Sunni, I'll need you to sign a few papers, and then we'll go over the list of medications," Dr. Voss said. "He's on a strong antibiotic and will need a dose of the pain medication every four to six hours for the next few days."

"Every four to six hours?" Aiden hiked a brow at his mom. "You're going to have to run back and forth to the shelter to give the dog a pill?"

"Of course not, sweetheart." Sunni gave him a bright smile. "He'll be at the house for a few days."

At the house.

Aiden should have known.

"You can take a seat in the waiting room, Aiden," Dr. Voss said. "It won't take very long."

After they left, Aiden approached the crate cautiously and bent down. A pair of bottomless, espresso-brown eyes stared back at him.

The dog was a mix of some sort. Coonhound and Labrador retriever, maybe, with a pointed nose, floppy ears and a tail hinged in the middle like a broken windshield wiper. It was also thin to the point of emaciation, with uneven patches of gray and brown bristles instead of fur. Even at the peak of health it wouldn't be the adorable, cuddly kind of pup most people wanted to adopt.

"You know what Sunni is up to, right?" Aiden whispered. "We're both invalids, and she's hoping we bond during our convalescence."

The dog bared its teeth and growled.

Aiden nodded. "I totally agree."

Chapter Five

Mondays.

Maddie decided there were times they deserved their reputation.

She clicked the mouse and brought up slide number twelve, even though she was fairly certain she'd lost the teenagers at number four.

Tyler's eyes were glued to his cell phone, Skye was drawing on the cover of her notebook and Justin appeared to be napping.

But at least they were here. Maddie had expected to spend Monday evening catching up on her emails, but the teens had drifted into the conference room one at a time and claimed their seats at the table.

The high school guidance counselor had given Maddie the link for the career assessment survey, so they'd spent the first hour in the computer lab, filling out the questionnaire. She planned to go over the results at their next session, but there were still twenty minutes left in this one.

I could use some help here, Lord.

No sooner than Maddie sent up the silent prayer, Aiden limped into the room.

"The door was unlocked again." He claimed the empty chair at the table as if it had been reserved especially for him.

As if he hadn't been a no-show on Saturday afternoon, even though Maddie had stayed an extra hour—or two—waiting for him.

Aiden's decision not to follow up on his request for help didn't surprise Maddie. What *did* surprise her was the disappointment that had clung like a burr on her favorite cardigan for the rest of the day.

She hadn't seen him at New Life Fellowship on Sunday morning, either. Maddie served in the church nursery twice a month, and by the time the last set of parents had picked up their child, everyone had left the building.

She'd told herself it was for the best, but here he was again. And once more, the teenagers were giving Aiden their full attention.

Maddie set down the clicker and went with it.

"Aiden, what was the topic of your senior presentation?"

"My senior presentation?"

She nodded. "You were a year ahead of me in high school, and *I* had to give one, so I'm pretty sure you did, too."

"Maybe he skipped that day," Tyler interjected.

The gleam in the boy's eye told Maddie he was contemplating it, too.

"It wouldn't matter." Skye slid lower in her chair. "They just make you do it the next day."

"What if he hadn't come back the next day?" Tyler retorted. "Or the next? What if he hadn't come back at all?"

Why did Maddie get the feeling that Tyler wasn't talking about Aiden anymore?

Skye tossed her mane of brown-and-lavender-striped hair. "Then he would've been stupid—"

"Survival camping."

Skye and Tyler, who were glaring at each other across the table, spun toward Aiden.

"What's that?" Skye blurted.

"You go into the woods with nothing more than you can carry in a backpack," Aiden explained. "You find your own water. Food. Make a shelter to sleep in."

The girl's eyes widened. "That's crazy."

"The faculty board thought so, too." Aiden grinned. "But I still got an A."

"It sounds like one of those shows on TV," Tyler said. "I saw one episode where a guy climbed into a hollow tree and it was full of wasps. He got stung, like, a thousand times."

Aiden shrugged. "I didn't have to worry about bugs. It was February."

He'd gone camping. In February. On purpose.

"Where did you sleep?" Justin unexpectedly joined the conversation. Maddie grabbed onto the back of a chair for support.

"I made a snow cave. Snow is actually a great insulator." Aiden dropped his voice a notch. "That's why you don't see bears putting on sweaters before they go into hibernation."

Skye giggled.

Giggled.

Justin had spoken up, Skye was acting seventeen instead of twenty-seven and Tyler was actually looking at Aiden instead of his cell phone.

And Maddie? She was a little in awe—and a whole lot of envious—at how effortlessly Aiden had connected with the three teenagers.

"You're supposed to write an outline and do research and stuff." Tyler tossed an accusing look at Maddie, as if she were the one who'd written the guidelines for their senior presentation.

Aiden laughed. "You don't think I did some research before I ventured into the woods when it was only ten degrees outside?"

Tyler crossed his arms, covering his interest with a skeptical look. "They really let you talk about camping?"

"I didn't just talk," Aiden said. "I brought in my backpack and showed them how I made it through the weekend with the supplies I'd packed. Like Maddie said, the whole idea behind the senior presentation is to learn more about something that interests you…and in the process maybe learn something about yourself."

At least someone remembered what Maddie had said during their study session the previous week. She just hadn't expected it to be Aiden.

An alarm chirped, and Tyler reached for his backpack. "I gotta go," he mumbled.

"Hold on a second." Maddie decided it was time to take control of the conversation again. "Does anyone have any questions before our next meeting?"

She was greeted with silence.

"All right… I'll see you at six thirty this Friday."

They all grabbed their things and bolted for the door.

Everyone except Aiden. He raised the hand that wasn't in the cast.

"I have a question. How do we find my sister?"

Maddie gripped the back of the chair again to counteract the unexpected weakness in her knees.

"But I…when you didn't show up on Saturday, I thought you'd changed your mind." The words came out in a rush, and the light in Aiden's eyes disappeared as swiftly as the sun on a winter afternoon.

"No one in my family had a reason to come into town that day," he said after a moment.

And Aiden couldn't drive.

Maddie realized how difficult it must be for such an independent man to rely on others—even his own family—for help. Which made the fact that Aiden had returned to the library to enlist hers a little scary.

"Anna had to finish up an order tonight and get it ready for shipment, so I hitched a ride with her," Aiden continued. "Bracelets…not ice cream, just in case you were wondering."

Maddie didn't know Anna Leighton very well—she'd been several years ahead of Maddie in school—but it was common knowledge the young widow had converted the second floor of The Happy Cow, her family-owned ice-cream shop, into a combination studio and boutique where she designed and sold a unique line of nature-inspired jewelry.

It was also common knowledge that Liam Kane had proposed to Anna a few weeks ago.

Maddie had overheard a group of women talking about how excited Sunni Mason was that two of her adopted sons had found love.

"Only one more to go," one of them had said.

"I have a feeling Sunni will have a long wait with Aiden," came her friend's laughing response. "I'm not sure there's a woman fast enough to catch that boy. Not that they haven't tried, mind you."

Maddie was used to people speaking freely in front of her. She was a permanent fixture in the library—like her desk or a lamp—and everyone seemed to forget she was there.

Still, Maddie didn't want to analyze too closely why the details of that whispered conversation had been stored away, when so many others had slipped from her mind.

"Can you post this on your community message board?" Aiden dipped his hand into his jacket pocket and pulled out a piece of paper. "I had to come up with a legitimate excuse for turning down Anna's rocky road sundae."

Maddie glanced down at the flier. The top half gave detailed information about River Quest, and underneath the dotted line was a registration form for those adventurous enough to sign up.

Suddenly, Aiden's words sank in. "Your family doesn't know you're looking for your sister?"

Something dark flashed in Aiden's eyes. "They know I *promised* I would…they just don't know I started yet."

Aiden was relieved when Maddie didn't press him further and ask why. Not when he wasn't sure of the answer himself.

All Aiden knew was that he couldn't fail and disappoint his family. Just once, he wanted to be the hero who swooped in and saved people from trouble instead of the one causing it.

Maddie pulled her chair out from the table. "I… I'll need some basic background information from you, and we can go from there."

"Now?"

Aiden's question seemed to surprise her. "Isn't that why you're here?"

"Yeah, but I thought we'd be setting up another day and time to meet," he said slowly. "You worked all day and then had to spend the evening with Dallas and Ponyboy—"

"Aiden!" Maddie clapped a hand over her mouth but couldn't quite suppress the laughter that backlit her beautiful green eyes. Beautiful green eyes that narrowed with suspicion a split second later. "Wait a second. You said you don't read. *The Outsiders* is a classic."

"There's a book, too?" Aiden cocked his head, careful to keep his expression neutral. "I thought it was just a movie."

He waited for the look of horror or pity, but the suspicion only deepened, which kind of took the fun out of teasing her.

Aiden had figured out at an early age that people didn't think he had a lot going on upstairs. He wasn't like his brothers. Brendan could crunch numbers and decipher complicated spreadsheets, and in his spare time, Liam could assemble a rocket from a box of spare parts.

In one of his Sunday morning messages, Pastor Seth had told the congregation that God gave all His children unique gifts. For Aiden, though, finding those gifts felt more like combing the grass for Easter eggs rather than spotting a brightly wrapped present under the tree on Christmas morning.

In other words, he was still looking.

"I don't mind starting tonight." Maddie pulled out the chair next to his and sat down, stirring the air—and Aiden's senses—with the scent of lily of the valley. He recognized the fragrance because the flowers appeared every spring. They weren't showy like Sunni's roses or the hydrangeas that bloomed along the foundation of the house. Lily of the valley blossoms were small and delicate. Easily overlooked. But if a person was paying attention, the flowers were surprisingly strong, brightening the shadowy places in the yard and thriving where others would have faded away.

"Aiden?"

He hadn't been paying attention. "Sorry." Aiden shifted restlessly, rattling the joints of the high-backed wooden chair. No doubt the conference room was a cozy, comfortable place to hold a meeting, but at this time of night, the pain from his injuries would normally have already forced him to the couch. "What's your first question?"

"What is your sister's name?"

"I don't know." Aiden pushed the words out through gritted teeth.

"But..." Maddie paused and searched his face. "How can you find your sister if you don't know her name."

"That's why I asked *you* for help."

"Okay..." Maddie drew in a breath. Released it again.

"We'll do what we always do when we're not sure where to start, then."

"Dive in headfirst?"

"Ask God for direction."

"Ask God."

Aiden shouldn't have been stunned by Maddie's suggestion. She was a believer. Attended church every Sunday, just like he did. But the fact that prayer hadn't crossed Aiden's mind showed how far he'd drifted from God since the accident.

He tried. He really did. But Aiden didn't know what to say—and he wasn't sure God was listening. In his darkest moments, Aiden wasn't sure God cared about the details of his life at all. If He did, where had He been the night Aiden had ended up in the ditch, leaving both his body and his plans for River Quest temporarily out of commission?

An all-knowing God had to know how important the competition was to him.

But Aiden flashed a smile at Maddie, because he battled those unsettling doubts the same way he'd been battling his pain.

Alone.

"That's a good idea."

Maddie released the breath she hadn't realized she'd been holding when Aiden agreed.

A swatch of ink-black hair slid over his forehead, veiling his expression as he bowed his head.

The hum of the furnace was the only sound in the room and Aiden didn't seem inclined to break it, so Maddie was the one who asked for direction and wisdom. She tacked on a silent prayer for Aiden's healing—of the body and mind—before she closed with a heartfelt but expectant amen.

And opened her eyes to find Aiden looking at *her*

expectantly. Without the patch, Maddie got a close-up view of the jagged cuts that fanned out from his eye.

"Not very pretty, but at least it still works." Aiden winked at her to prove it.

Maddie was mortified he'd caught her staring. Maybe her dad was right. Maybe it wasn't a good idea to be alone with a man in the library.

"If you don't know your sister's name," she managed to stammer, "then we'll start with her birthday."

"I'm not sure of that, either." A muscle worked in Aiden's jaw. "Brendan overheard our mom talking to a caseworker, but she'd hidden her pregnancy from everyone. He had no idea how far along she was at the time. She could have just found out she was pregnant or been about to give birth, for all we know."

"How old were you at the time?"

"About three, according to my brother."

That gave them a timeline to work with anyway. "What are your parents' names?"

"Carla Kane..." Aiden paused.

Maddie jotted that down. "And your father?"

"Darren Kane." The temperature in the room seemed to plummet from toasty to single digits when Aiden said the name. "But he was a long-distance truck driver, and he and my mom...things were never good between them. They split up a few times before they finally divorced."

"Oh." Maddie jotted that down only because she needed a moment to fit that piece together with what she already knew about Aiden's background. Her heart twisted at the thought of what his home life had been like before he and his brothers had moved to Castle Falls.

"And no, I can't contact them and ask what happened to our sister." He'd anticipated Maddie's next question. "Darren went off the grid after the divorce and Carla..."

Aiden's jaw tightened. "A friend of hers sent Sunni a letter when I was fourteen, letting us know she'd passed away."

"Aiden…I'm so sorry." No matter what Aiden's relationship with his biological mother had—or hadn't—been, finding out about her death that way would have been difficult.

"Apparently Carla got sick, but she refused to go to the hospital to find out what was wrong. Her appendix ruptured and the infection spread through her body. She wasn't in the best of health to begin with." Aiden picked up a pen and tapped it against the table. "She was living in Grand Rapids at the time, so the funeral and burial were there."

Aiden's expression didn't change, but in the erratic drumbeat of the pen she heard the emotion he couldn't—or wouldn't—express.

"Did you go?" Maddie resisted the urge to reach for his hand. She was venturing into unfamiliar territory, where any misstep could result in Aiden walking out the door.

He reminded Maddie of the river he loved. Below the surface of Aiden's roguish smile and easygoing charm were hidden depths as inviting as they were unpredictable. Especially for a girl who'd never learned how to swim.

"We couldn't. Trish Jenkins—that was her friend—didn't get around to sending the letter for six months."

Maddie questioned the sensitivity of someone who hadn't given Aiden and his brothers the opportunity to say goodbye to their biological mother, but she kept her feelings to herself.

"Where were you and your brothers born?"

Aiden told her the name of the hospital, and Maddie nodded. Finally. Something she could work with. "I'll search for adoption agencies downstate and see what pops up."

"Brendan did say that whoever Carla was talking to that day mentioned a closed adoption."

Maddie struggled to maintain a neutral expression as she wrote that down, but she must not have been successful because Aiden leaned forward.

"You're sure you want to take this on? There's still time to back out."

I was in the middle before I knew that I had begun.

The quote from Jane Austen's *Pride and Prejudice* zipped through Maddie's mind, even though Aiden Kane was more rakish swashbuckler than brooding aristocrat.

And you, my dear Maddie, are a wallflower, remember?

An old-fashioned term but one that fit a quiet girl who loved vintage clothing and tended to blend in with her surroundings. Aiden might not have noticed her, but that didn't change the fact that he *needed* her.

"I'm not backing out," Maddie said.

"Okay." The genuine relief on Aiden's face washed away any lingering doubts Maddie had about taking on such an unusual request. "What do you typically charge people for something like this?"

"There's no charge. I'm the librarian, remember?"

Aiden Kane was no different from anyone else who came into the library. Helping him was simply part of her job.

But when Aiden smiled again, Maddie suspected she was going to have to remind herself of that often.

Chapter Six

Aiden's pain pill was wearing off.

It was the only thing that would explain his sudden, inexplicable urge to count the number of pale gold freckles scattered across Maddie's nose.

"I'd better go." He pushed to his feet, ignoring the pain that bloomed in his knee. Over the weekend, it had dropped from an eight to a seven, so Aiden supposed the physical therapist's claim that he was slowly improving was accurate. The "slowly" part was, anyway.

He pressed his hip into the back of the chair for balance, not wanting Maddie to know he was paying the price for rejecting her suggestion they move to the more comfortable chairs in the reading nook.

She already knew too much.

Maddie probably thought she'd done a good job hiding her thoughts, but every emotion from shock to disbelief had been reflected in her eyes when Aiden had told her about his parents.

No doubt Maddie had grown up in a stable home, sheltered and loved, while details of his life were the opposite of those feel-good, made-for-cable movies that Sunni liked to watch on the weekends.

Aiden had officially lived with their adoptive mom longer than the woman who'd raised him, but even though the memories had faded, there was no denying the first ten years of his life had formed a thick layer of scar tissue around his heart.

Aiden tried not to dwell on the past, but he hadn't realized how difficult it would be to take a trip back in time.

He still wasn't sure he wanted a companion for the journey, either.

Aiden glanced down at Maddie when she followed him into the hallway.

Once again, she was wearing a dress that looked like it had come straight from another time period. Brown might have looked drab on anyone else, but the color set off Maddie's vivid green eyes while a velvet belt drew attention to her tiny waist. Aiden wondered if the style was a personal preference or standard protocol for librarians, like the way Maddie wore her hair.

He suddenly noticed the bright yellow pencil poking out from the ever-present bun, and he scraped his hand across his jaw to cover a smile.

"We should exchange phone numbers," he blurted.

Maddie froze midstep. Pivoted to face him. "Why?"

Not the response Aiden usually got when he asked a girl for her number. But then, he didn't usually blurt the words, either.

"So we can set up another time to get together?"

Maddie frowned.

Again, not the typical response.

She'd claimed research was part of her job. It made sense that Maddie would prefer to meet with him during the library's regular business hours. Maybe her hesitation was due to the fact that people in Castle Falls had a tendency to get into each other's business.

"I get it. If we're seen together during your free time,

the rumor mill will have us planning a double wedding with Liam and Anna on Christmas Eve."

Twin spots of color bloomed in Maddie's cheeks. "That's not what… I thought you wanted me to gather information and start the search."

"I do. But you're going to need me, too." Aiden planned to wring as many details out of Brendan as he could. As much as he loved his oldest brother, a tiny sliver of resentment had worked its way under Aiden's skin when he'd found out Brendan had withheld something so important from him.

Aiden was the youngest in the family, but they were all adults now. He wanted Brendan to see him as an equal, not a child who needed to be protected from the truth.

"Okay." Maddie drew out the word. "What day of the week will work for you?"

"Other than PT appointments twice a week, my calendar is wide open." Aiden smiled to prove he was handling the forced inactivity just fine, thank you very much.

"There are a lot of interruptions while I'm here during the day, which is why I schedule meetings with the students after regular business hours." Maddie nibbled on her lower lip. "I suppose it would be best if we did, too."

"Give me your phone and I'll add my number to your contacts. You can text me with a day and time, and I'll make it work."

Maddie reached into the pocket of her dress, extracted her cell and reluctantly handed it over. The screensaver photo was a panoramic view of the Grand Canyon.

"Sweet view." He typed in his name and number. "You've been to the Grand Canyon?"

"Yes… I mean, no." Maddie plucked the phone from his hand.

"So which is it?"

"Both."

Aiden lifted a brow. "I don't understand."

"Don't worry." The elusive dimple made an appearance. "You wouldn't be the first."

Aiden didn't have time to dwell on the meaning behind the cryptic statement because Maddie took cover behind the circulation desk.

The not-so-subtle hint was something Aiden *did* understand.

"Night." He clumped slowly toward the door, trying not to put too much weight on his bad leg and wincing every time his crutch scraped the surface of the hardwood floor. He glanced over his shoulder and caught Maddie watching, her forehead puckered in concern. "Which way to the bell tower again, mademoiselle?"

Before Maddie could question his reference to *The Hunchback of Notre Dame*, Aiden ducked his head to hide a grin and let the door snap shut behind him.

Maddie had taken three laps around the circulation desk before she realized that Aiden Kane had turned her into a...a *pacer.*

She veered toward the beverage station in the reading nook to brew a cup of lemon tea and spotted a ball of wadded-up paper on the floor. One look at the black roses climbing up the margins, and Maddie knew the artist was Skye.

She collapsed into the closest chair. There were times a cup of tea provided a certain amount of comfort, and then were those moments when a girl knew the only thing that would bring peace was turning to the One who comforted the soul.

Lord, I don't know Skye very well, but I can tell she's angry. Hurting.

All three of them were.

Skye, who drew her feelings on the cover of her notebook. Storm clouds and raindrops and flowers that bloomed on chains instead of vines. Tyler's fists were always clenched, as if he were ready for a fight. Justin, on the other hand, chose to stay underneath the radar, never voicing an opinion or a complaint.

For a fleeting moment, Maddie considered admitting defeat. Why donate several evenings a week to students who seemed to have given up before they'd even started?

Maybe they're quick to give up because people have given up on them.

The thought struck Maddie square in the heart, and she dropped her forehead to her knees.

Okay, Lord, I'm in. But You're going to have to help me out. I didn't relate very well to teenagers even when I was *one.*

And something told Maddie the outline she usually followed wasn't going to work this time.

She'd have to think outside the box.

The career assessment survey had been a useful tool in the past, but Maddie suspected the results wouldn't generate any of the curiosity and enthusiasm she'd seen the teenagers display when Aiden had talked about survival camping.

Maddie admired the way he'd designed his senior project to dovetail with the gifts and unique abilities God had hardwired into him.

A thought so unexpected—and daring—pushed Maddie out of her comfortable chair and onto her feet.

Why couldn't her three students do the same?

No one had said their meetings had to be confined to the conference room in the library. Instead of thinking outside the box, what if Maddie took them outside the box?

What if…

Maddie's shoe caught the rug next to the children's area.

Ack. She'd been pacing again.

Maddie stopped, but thoughts continued to swirl inside her head.

Tyler and Justin and Skye needed more than a passing grade on their senior presentation. They needed to succeed. Needed to feel like they belonged.

Maddie leaned against a bookcase for support as the thoughts converged into one daring—or maybe the word was *deranged*—idea.

They needed…Aiden.

Aiden ignored the crosswalk at the end of the block and cut through the middle of the street.

A harvest moon had risen above the trees and cast everything in a pale, shimmery gold that reminded him of Maddie's hair.

Yup. He definitely needed that pain pill.

Aiden had almost reached The Happy Cow when a squad car rounded the corner. A spotlight on top of the vehicle captured Aiden in its reach.

The driver's-side window rolled down.

"Aiden Kane?"

"Yes." Aiden narrowed his eyes, not recognizing either the voice or the face of the man behind the wheel.

"I thought so." The deputy hopped out of the squad car and extended his hand. "Carter Bristow."

Underneath the streetlight, Aiden could see the deputy was about Liam's age, with dark brown hair cropped close to his head and skin stained bronze from the summer sun.

Bristow didn't look like the kind of guy who whiled away the weekends working on his tan, so Aiden guessed he spent them in a kayak or clinging to the side of a cliff. The guy's ramrod-straight posture and no-nonsense expression hinted at a few tours in the armed services, too.

"It's nice to meet you?" Aiden hadn't meant to pose it in the form of a question, but he wasn't sure what he'd done to warrant an impromptu meet and greet with one of the county's finest.

The deputy's gaze raked over him, taking a brief but thorough inventory of Aiden's injuries.

"Looks like you're on the mend," he said. "When I saw the truck, I figured you'd be leaving the scene in a body bag, not on a stretcher."

Apparently Deputy Carter Bristow didn't believe in sugarcoating things.

Aiden knew the pickup was totaled, but he hadn't seen the extent of the damage yet. His brothers had had it towed to the local garage where Frank, Castle Falls' friendly mechanic, had pronounced it dead on arrival.

Technically, the pickup wasn't Aiden's personal vehicle. It belonged to the business, which meant their insurance premiums would go up.

Yet another reason Aiden wanted to prove the accident hadn't been his fault.

"You were on duty the night of the accident?" Aiden had been told that almost every first responder within a twenty-five-mile radius had shown up at the scene.

"That's right."

"I was hoping I would have a chance to thank everyone who showed up that night," Aiden said. "I don't remember much after my truck hit the ditch."

"Is that why you requested a copy of my report?"

"Your report?" Aiden had been on heavy pain meds in the hospital, but he knew this wasn't the officer who'd taken his statement the next day.

"I was the first officer at the scene." Bristow gestured toward the squad car. "What do you say we step into my office for a few minutes?"

"Sure." What else *could* he say?

And why did he get the feeling the deputy wasn't happy with him? Was there some kind of protocol Aiden hadn't followed? Had he crossed some invisible blue line and offended the officer?

Aiden waved to get his future sister-in-law's attention through the window and held up two fingers.

Anna smiled and held up an ice-cream scoop, meaning he was going to get the rocky road sundae she'd promised him.

Aiden slid into the passenger seat and waited for the deputy to get in.

"So that's what you were looking for in the report?" Carter turned his radio down. "The names of the people who responded to the scene?"

"No." Thanks to Sunni, the importance of honesty was ingrained in Aiden, but he still had to push the word out.

"Can I ask what you *were* looking for?"

"The truth."

"The truth." Bristow's expression didn't change, but the set of his jaw did.

Okay, that hadn't come out quite the way Aiden had intended.

This was the deputy who'd done the reconstruction. The one who'd written "no skid marks" at the bottom of the report. If Aiden hadn't offended the deputy by requesting a copy of the report, he was well on his way if Deputy Bristow thought his integrity as well as his training was being called into question.

"I know *you* told the truth," Aiden said. "And it's not that I doubt your ability to do your job. I asked for a copy of the report because I was hoping there would be something there that backed up my side of the story, too."

Carter studied him for a moment. "You claimed there was another vehicle involved."

"There was. A truck came around the corner in my lane—"

"How do you know it was a truck?"

Aiden blinked. How *did* he know the vehicle barreling toward him had been a truck?

"The lights were shining directly into my eyes," he said slowly. "If it had been a car, they would have been lower."

"And you think the driver ran you off the road and then kept going?"

"I *know* they did. I'm just not sure if it was on purpose."

Carter's eyes narrowed. "Even if it wasn't, you're talking about a pretty serious crime. And unless an eyewitness, or the perpetrator himself, comes forward, almost impossible to prove."

"I know everyone believes I took the corner too fast—" Everyone including Aiden's own brothers. "But I'm not making this up to cover my own mistake—"

"Aiden." Carter held up his hand, cutting him off midsentence. "I said it would be almost impossible to prove. Not that I don't believe you."

Chapter Seven

On Friday, Maddie's car rattled over the wooden bridge that linked the main road to Sunni Mason's property.

A year ago, after a hiatus that had started after Rich Mason's death and stretched over the next decade, Castle Falls Outfitters had started to offer guided river trips again. Everyone in Castle Falls was ecstatic, of course, and even Pastor Tamblin had scheduled a Sunday afternoon outing for the congregation, but Maddie hadn't taken advantage of the opportunity to hop into a canoe and paddle down the river.

The towering pines that lined the road made her feel even smaller. Unlike a book, the wilderness was too big to hold in her hands.

Like the Grand Canyon.

Maddie's cheeks burned at the memory. Of course Aiden would assume she'd taken the photograph on her screensaver. It's what everyone else would do—preserve the memory of a place where they'd actually put boots on the ground, not a place they'd visited in the pages of a favorite novel.

Gravel crunched underneath the tires as Maddie followed the twists and turns of the rutted driveway. The scenery began to change as she rounded a corner, the trees thinning until they opened up completely and revealed a scattering of buildings in the spacious yard carved from the forest.

She drove past a large outbuilding with a red canoe painted on the side and a charming log cabin tucked in a stand of birch. An older home, modest but well-maintained, overlooked the river, its stone foundation hemmed in bright yellow mums that matched the color of the front door.

"Is this it?" Skye, who'd been silent on the drive from town, yanked out the earbuds attached to her cell phone and pressed her nose against the passenger-side window.

"This is it." Maddie claimed an empty spot in front of a two-story garage and put the car in Park.

It hadn't been difficult to convince the teenagers to replace their scheduled session with a field trip right after school let out for the day. Maddie had called the principal asking for permission earlier that morning and was told that since Maddie was meeting with the seniors after hours, it was up to her when—and where—the study sessions took place.

"Doesn't look like anyone's here." Tyler, who also hadn't said a word since he'd climbed into Maddie's car, spoke up from the back seat.

"They heard we were coming and took off," Skye joked.

The boys didn't laugh, though, and Maddie realized it was because they'd been thinking the same thing.

I hope this will work, God.

Because now that the teenagers were here, Maddie was beginning to doubt the wisdom of her plan.

"Can we get out, Miss Montgomery?" Skye was already opening her door.

"Of course." Maddie summoned a smile and turned off the engine.

The teens formed a line behind Maddie and trailed behind her as she walked up the narrow sidewalk to the front door.

It swung open before she got there.

"Maddie." Sunni Mason, a striking woman in her mid to late fifties, wore a white apron emblazoned with the words Hug the Cook and a smile that expanded to include the three teenagers skulking in the background. "Come in, come in. Aiden will be so happy to have some company."

Maddie blinked. How had Sunni known that Aiden was the person she'd come to see?

"I just pulled out a pan of cinnamon rolls for our Saturday morning breakfast, but I always make a few extra if someone wants a late-night snack." Sunni shepherded them down the hall and into a spacious kitchen, where the scent of cinnamon and vanilla hung in the air.

Tyler and Justin practically started salivating when they spotted the platter of warm baked goods on the butcher-block island.

"Right through those doors, Maddie." Sunni pointed to the French doors on the opposite side of the kitchen. "You go on, and I'll see if I can't round up a few people to taste-test this batch of rolls."

Maddie expected the teenagers to balk at being left with a stranger, but they didn't even glance at Maddie as Aiden's mom nudged them toward the table.

Maddie's fingers trembled as she reached for the handle on the door and pushed it open. Two shaggy heads swiveled toward her. One belonged to Aiden, the other to a dog curled up underneath a wicker chair next to the sofa Aiden was lying on.

And in spite of what Sunni had claimed, neither one of them looked happy to see her.

The glass wall of the sunroom framed a stunning view of the river, but Maddie couldn't tear her gaze from Aiden.

The bruises had almost disappeared and the cuts had

faded, but Maddie saw something in Aiden's expression that instantly sparked her concern. Or maybe it was what she *didn't* see. The perpetual gleam of mischief in the cobalt-blue eyes was hidden behind the shadows that had collected there.

Instead of faded jeans and the usual flannel, Aiden wore sweatpants, a wrinkled T-shirt and two days' growth of beard. A wooden checkerboard, stacks of DVDs and a plate of chocolate chip cookies on the coffee table provided evidence that Aiden's family had been trying to make his forced convalescence more bearable.

"Maddie." Aiden started to push to his feet, and then sank back into the cushions when pain from the sudden movement apparently pushed back. "What are you doing here?"

"I..." She glanced down at the dog. The bristles on its back quivered like the quills on an irritated porcupine. If the animal could speak, Maddie had no doubt it would echo Aiden's question.

"You found something already?" Aiden gripped the arm of the couch and he leaned forward, his eyes locked on her face.

Maddie mentally kicked herself. Four days had passed since he'd given her a few clues into his family history. Of course Aiden would assume she'd come with news about his sister.

"Not yet, but I've been compiling a list of adoption agencies in Michigan." There were a lot more than Maddie had expected to find, but she wasn't going to mention that yet. Or that her initial search for information regarding closed adoptions hadn't been encouraging.

"I'm actually here—" *deep breath, Maddie* "—to drop off a registration form."

Aiden frowned. "Registration form?"

"For River Quest."

* * *

Aiden couldn't have heard Maddie right.

His gaze swept over her slim frame. A strand of pearls glowed against Maddie's black velvet—*velvet*—dress, and the shoes on her feet reminded him of something a ballerina might wear.

She was absolutely enchanting. Absolutely out of her mind.

Or maybe Aiden was experiencing some strange, residual injury from the accident that had affected his hearing.

"Did you…" He cleared his throat. "Say River Quest?"

Maddie's brisk nod set a tendril of tawny hair free from its captivity. "Yes."

Aiden would have laughed out loud if the serious look in those wide green eyes hadn't told him that she was, well, completely serious.

"It isn't a leisurely paddle down the river, Maddie," he felt obligated to remind her, although the article in the newspaper had made that pretty clear. "It's an obstacle course."

A *challenging* obstacle course, mentally and physically, that tested both strength and endurance. Aiden had designed it that way. He'd led multiple excursions for New Life Fellowship's young singles group over the past few years and couldn't remember Maddie Montgomery joining in on any of them.

"I realize that." As if she'd read his mind, Maddie's spine straightened. "I'm not actually going to be part of the team, though," she continued. "I'm the…sponsor."

"Okay." Aiden's relief distilled into curiosity. "Who *is* on the team, then?"

Maddie's gaze slid away from him, and Aiden grew suspicious when she parried his question with one of her own.

"What's your dog's name?"

"Dodger."

"Ah." Maddie smiled. "A baseball fan."

Aiden didn't correct her, even though the name had nothing to do with baseball. It did, however, perfectly fit an animal that could barely walk and yet somehow managed to collect things—stray socks and paper napkins and occasionally the TV remote—and stash them behind the rocking chair in the corner.

"It's nice to meet you, Dodger." Maddie reached down to pet the dog, and Aiden almost strangled himself on his next breath.

"Maddie, don't—"

Too late. She smoothed a hand over Dodger's rough fur, her fingers gently tracing a path between the squares of white bandages that covered the dog's side like a patchwork quilt.

Dodger made a sound deep in his throat, and his top lip curled back.

Aiden had been on the receiving end of more than a few snarls since Sunni had forced them into becoming roommates, so he knew what one looked like. But this baring of the teeth looked more like a...*smile.* And Dodger's whiplike tail? Definitely wagging.

Go figure.

Maddie gave the dog one more pat before she straightened and looked at Aiden again.

"Was Dodger in the truck with you when it happened?"

It took a moment for Aiden to realize Maddie was referring to the accident.

"No." But now that he thought about it, they'd both been injured because someone was too cowardly to step forward and own up to what they'd done. "And technically he isn't my dog. Sunni is taking care of him until his incision heals, and then he's going up for adoption."

"So you're keeping each other company."

"That's one way of putting it." In reality, it was more

like a self-imposed exile. He and Dodger had holed up together in the sunroom for the better part of the week, growling at each other and everyone who walked through the door.

Before the accident, Brendan and Liam would have tossed Aiden into his canoe and told him that he could come back when he stopped acting like a jerk. Now they smiled patiently and fluffed his pillow instead of smothering him with it.

Aiden didn't want to take out his frustration on his family, but at his appointment on Tuesday, his doctor had refused to give him the green light to resume his normal activities.

"We both know you'll go pedal to the metal if I drop the flag, son," he'd told Aiden. "So it's my recommendation you spend a few more weeks in the pit."

Not only was Dr. Wallis a die-hard car racing fan, he'd been the Kanes' family physician since Aiden was ten years old. Aiden had been in his office so many times, the doctor had laughingly told Sunni that Aiden should have his own examination room.

The doctor's orders had snuffed out the flicker of hope Aiden had been tending that he could be more involved in River Quest.

A burst of laughter drifted from the kitchen, and Aiden frowned. Sunni's kitchen was always open, but she hadn't mentioned there were people coming over.

Unless…

He glanced at Maddie. A smile played at the corners of her lips, and Aiden realized that Sunni wasn't feeding company. She was feeding Maddie's mystery team.

"You mentioned you're the sponsor…but who is actually going to attempt the course?" He chose the word *attempt* on purpose.

"Some high school seniors I've been meeting with,"

Maddie said, triggering the strong sense of foreboding that usually preceded a flashback of Aiden's accident. "They aren't in sports or any extracurricular activities, and the only time I've ever seen them look interested in *anything* was when you talked about your senior presentation… and River Quest. So I put two and two together, and here we are."

"Hold on." An image of the boys in the library conference room flashed in Aiden's mind. One surly, one silent. Both with spaghetti arms. Attitude. "You aren't talking about The Outsiders, are you?"

"Aiden!" Maddie choked out—and then confirmed his suspicions with a quick glance at the door. "Their names are Tyler and Justin."

"It's a great idea—" *Not.* "But the deadline to register was today."

"That's why I wanted to make sure I dropped it off right away this morning. I called and talked to Lily, and she said that technically the cutoff would be midnight tonight."

Thank you, Lily.

Aiden tried another approach. "Aren't you supposed to be helping them with their senior projects?"

"Yes, but that's the best part. This *will* help them. The high school guidance counselor said they're barely passing their classes." Maddie's voice had dropped a notch. "They need something to boost their confidence."

And she'd chosen *River Quest*?

Aiden tried to figure out a way to let Maddie down gently. When nothing came to mind, he figured he would have to come up with a plan that would save Maddie from acute disappointment, and two teenage boys from public humiliation.

"Okay, I'll meet you outside the Trading Post in five minutes," Aiden said. "It's in the pole building next to Liam's workshop. You'll see the sign on the door."

"Five minutes." Maddie's dimple made an appearance, and Aiden felt a stab of guilt.

The moment she was out of sight, Dodger whined.

"I know, I know," Aiden shot back. "But I don't remember asking for your opinion." He grabbed his denim shirt and tried to shake the wrinkles out. Nope. Not happening. They'd settled into the fabric and refused to budge. Kind of like the way Aiden had stubbornly refused to move from the couch the past few days. If Dr. Wallis wanted him to hang around the pit for a few more weeks…

Aiden suddenly noticed the area surrounding the couch *was* a pit.

"Do you think she noticed?"

Dodger's straggly eyebrows lifted.

"Yeah. Me, too." Aiden slipped the shirt on and tugged the sleeve over his cast. "Don't steal the remote when I'm gone."

To his astonishment, instead of ignoring him, Dodger staggered to his feet. And then the dog, who hadn't shown the least bit of interest in doing anything other than eating and sleeping and snapping at Aiden since they'd brought it home from the vet, followed him out the door.

The late-afternoon sunlight that filtered through the trees lacked power, but Aiden, who'd spent the entire day inside with shades pulled down, still had to adjust to its brightness.

He'd expected to see the two boys, but Maddie had brought along the girl with the purple stripes in her hair, too. The teenagers stood in a loose knot outside the door of the Trading Post, avoiding eye contact with Aiden and each other as Maddie stepped forward to make the formal introductions.

"Aiden, this is Skye Robinson."

He smiled even though he wasn't sure where the girl

fit in. The teams for River Quest were limited to two people. "It's nice to meet you, Skye."

She mumbled a response, arms crossed, already shivering in a thin T-shirt, skinny jeans and high-heel suede boots.

"Tyler Olsen." Maddie gestured at the boy who'd been openly skeptical that Aiden had been allowed to "talk about camping" for his senior project. "And Justin Wagner."

Aiden nodded and extended his hand. After a moment's hesitation, each one of the boys reached out and shook it.

Uh-huh. Just as Aiden suspected. No upper-body strength whatsoever. And if they looked like they'd get winded climbing up a flight of stairs, the chances of them scaling Eagle Rock were pretty slim.

But they had to know it, too, which just might work in Aiden's favor.

Chapter Eight

Maddie's misgivings melted away when Tyler and Justin shook Aiden's hand.

So far, things were definitely working in her favor.

Aiden opened the door and waited for them to file inside the building he'd referred to as the Trading Post.

Maddie hadn't expected it to actually look like one.

Stacks of colorful wool trapper blankets filled a birch bark canoe in the corner, and old maps of the area decorated the walls above rough-hewn wooden shelves lined with souvenirs. The atmosphere was rustic and charming all at the same time.

"I didn't know you'd opened a store."

"I didn't," Aiden said. "The women in the family get the credit for that. When we decided to expand the business, Sunni and Lily took the word literally. Some of us were fine with asking people to sign in on a clipboard when they booked a day-trip or checked out equipment, but apparently this adds 'depth—'" he put air quotes around the word "—to the whole experience."

"I think the women in your family are right." Maddie paused to look at the tiny metal charms that filled each compartment of an old wooden type case. "Anna sells her jewelry here, too?"

"She calls them memory charms, but Brendan calls it strategic marketing because repeat guests can buy a new one every time they visit." Aiden grinned, and Maddie felt a strange little flutter in her chest.

Given her medical history, anything outside the ordinary, predictable rhythm of Maddie's heart would have been cause for alarm… Oh, who was she kidding? If Aiden was the reason that particular organ was skipping every other beat, it was *still* cause for alarm.

She wouldn't be one of the many women who'd succumbed to Aiden Kane's roughish smile.

Couldn't be.

Maddie picked up a silver charm shaped like an otter. "I think it's great that Anna is able to contribute something so special to the business."

The shadows Maddie had seen in his eyes when she'd come into the room returned even as he nodded in agreement. "She designed a special pin for River Quest, too."

Tyler gave the jewelry display a dismissive glance. "I'd rather have a T-shirt."

"You don't get a pin by signing up for the course. It's for the people who *finish* it." Aiden shuffled behind the counter and propped his crutch against the wall. "It starts out easy and gets more difficult as you go along. Some of the teams have been practicing for a month already. If you aren't in top physical shape, you'll be starting out with a disadvantage."

Justin glanced over his shoulder at the door as if he was planning a quick exit, and Maddie felt a stab of panic.

What was Aiden doing? If Maddie didn't know better, she'd think he was trying to discourage them from entering the competition.

"Well, we have a month to prepare, too." *Almost.* "And determination is a strength, too, isn't it, Aiden?"

"Determination," Aiden echoed under his breath.

"There are challenges in the water and on land." He yanked open a drawer and pulled out a folder. "Each team is made up of two people, but there are times when you'll have to separate during the course, so knowing how to communicate is as important as knowing the fastest way to climb Eagle Rock."

Tyler and Justin exchanged a skeptical look, which only fed into the doubts Maddie had been battling since they'd followed Aiden into the Trading Post. From what she'd witnessed, Tyler's preferred method of communication was a sneer or an eye roll, while Justin preferred not to communicate at all.

"We've got plenty of time to work on that, too," Maddie said brightly.

Aiden winced, and she wondered if he was in pain again.

"If you're under eighteen, your parents have to give their permission for you to take part in the event." He pulled a stack of waivers from the drawer and fanned them out on the counter.

No one took one.

Aiden's eyebrows shot up. "Change your mind already?"

"I'm eighteen," Tyler muttered.

Aiden turned to Justin. "What about you?"

The boy glanced at the door again, and Maddie waited. She'd brought Justin here, but now that Aiden had explained what they were getting into—in vivid detail—it was up to him to make a commitment.

"Dude." Tyler clapped Justin on the shoulder. "What are you waiting for?"

Justin hesitated a fraction of a second before grabbing the permission slip off the counter.

"So all we need now is a sponsorship form," Maddie told Aiden.

It seemed to take him an inordinately long time to locate the paperwork, but he finally handed her a sheet of paper. "The entry fee is fifty dollars. Cash or check, no credit cards."

Maddie reached for her purse. "Okay."

"And no refunds."

"I can't think of a reason we'd need one!" Maddie signed her name on the line and handed the form back to Aiden. "There. We're all set."

But she'd lost them again. Tyler had his phone out again and Justin was tracing a knothole in the plank floor with the scuffed toe of his tennis shoe.

Skye was the only one looking at Maddie, although *glaring* would have been a better description.

"I don't know why I'm here," she said. "The rules say there can only be two people on a team."

Tyler abandoned his game long enough to smirk at her. "You can be our cheerleader."

Skye's chin jutted forward. "Do I look like a cheerleader?"

"No," Tyler shot back. "You—"

"Could design the team flag," Maddie said before Tyler could tell Skye what she *did* look like.

The girl's chin lifted another notch. "Flag?"

"Aiden mentioned we needed one for the first challenge," Maddie reminded her. If Anna Leighton had found a way to use her creativity, she hoped Skye would take advantage of the opportunity, too.

Everyone looked at Aiden for confirmation, and he nodded. "After you find your way through the tunnel…the dark, narrow tunnel…the flags will be in the cave."

Honestly. Maddie thought he could have left out the "dark and narrow" part.

"I don't see why we can't just draw a skull and crossbones on a towel and call it good," Tyler grumbled.

Skye deflated right in front of Maddie's eyes. Two sections of tinted hair merged together, concealing her expression as her gaze dropped to the floor.

"You could," Aiden said slowly. "But the team with the most creative flag gets ten minutes cut off their total time."

Tyler and Justin exchanged a quick look, and Maddie wanted to point at them and shout, *Did you see that? Communication!*

"Ten minutes is ten minutes," Justin finally said, a not-so-subtle hint they needed all the help they could get.

Now they were thinking like a team.

"That's about how long it will take for me to design one," Skye said. "What am I supposed to do the rest of the time?"

Tyler flexed his biceps. "Follow us around and record our awesomeness?"

Maddie smiled. "Actually…that's not a bad idea."

Three—no, make that *four*—pairs of eyes widened in disbelief.

"Skye is creative and has an artistic eye," she said. "She could put together a video collage of the competition and work it into your senior presentation."

Skye twisted a strand of lilac hair around her finger. "I don't know…what if it doesn't turn out well? I've taken pictures, but I've never done anything like that before."

"Figuring out how becomes part of your research," Maddie told her.

Skye slanted a look at Aiden. "Like he did for survival camping?"

"Exactly like that." Maddie smiled. "In fact, Aiden's senior project inspired the idea that you form a team for River Quest."

For some reason, Aiden's plan to scare the teenagers out of participating in the competition was failing miserably. And he had a pretty good hunch that reason was a five-foot-two, green-eyed pixie. A pixie who, as crazy as it seemed, had been inspired by *him*.

If only Maddie knew the idea for Aiden's senior project had been born out of desperation, not inspiration.

Because his personality was more suited to wide-open spaces than a classroom, Aiden had struggled to maintain a C average all through high school. The required senior project, which involved reading, note taking and organizing those notes into something that made sense, had seemed so daunting that Aiden had announced at supper one night that he was going to quit school.

Sunni had listened like she always did, and Aiden knew from experience his adoptive mom would take time to pray before she shared her thoughts about his decision. His older brothers weren't that patient. Over the next few days, Brendan and Liam had badgered Aiden until he'd finally gone to Sunni and told her that he wanted to take a weekend camping trip so he could think. For Aiden, thinking always came easier when he was *moving*.

His mom had agreed with one condition. That Aiden research winter camping first and come up with a plan so she would be able to sleep at night.

Aiden was so thrilled she'd said yes, he'd spent another week preparing for the challenge.

After he'd successfully survived and returned home with stories about his adventures that had lasted long into the night, Sunni had casually mentioned over a cup of hot chocolate how interesting it was that Aiden had not only had fun, he'd combined everything required for his senior project. Research. Critical thinking. Sharing information. And the most important ingredient—one that couldn't be contained on a note card—passion for his topic.

Moms. So wise. So *sneaky*.

Kind of like someone else Aiden knew.

Maddie claimed the teenagers wanted to participate in River Quest, but even after Aiden had given them a reality check along with their permission forms, he doubted they knew what they were signing up for.

Tyler definitely had a competitive streak, but from what Aiden had seen, his skills were limited to the games he'd downloaded on his cell phone. And while Tyler wasn't afraid to voice an opinion or a complaint, Justin was the exact opposite. He rarely spoke at all. Aiden could tell Justin was listening, but he wore the hunted look of someone who'd stumbled into unfamiliar territory where he didn't belong.

Like Dodger.

Aiden glanced down at the dog, who'd planted himself on the floor next to Maddie's feet.

While he watched, she reached down and idly scratched the bare spot behind Dodger's misshapen ear. Dodger's eyes drifted closed, and Aiden felt an unexpected tug of jealousy.

Jealous. Of a dog.

What was happening to him?

Aiden deposited Maddie's money into the cash box and shut the lid with a little more force than was necessary. "Once I get Justin's permission form, you'll be all set."

"Thank you." Maddie didn't move.

"Unless…" Aiden almost hated to ask. "There's something else you need?"

"As a matter of fact, there is" came the bright response. "We'll need a canoe."

"Sure—"

"And a coach."

Aiden stared at Maddie. She didn't mean *him*. But the dimple in her cheek clearly said that yes, she did.

"I think that's a great idea."

Aiden—who thought the opposite—shot a glare at

Liam. He hadn't realized his brother had been on the other side of a very thin door, working in the shop.

Eavesdropping.

"It would be a conflict of interest," Aiden argued. "I *designed* the course."

"All the challenges are posted on the website," his brother pointed out. "It's not like you'd be giving away any secrets. And like you said, some of the teams have been getting in shape for a month."

"And speaking of *in shape*—" Aiden waved the hand that worked instead of the one cradled in the sling. "Does it look like I can help them?"

He hated to use his injuries as an excuse, but when a guy was backed into a corner, he had to use whatever weapons were in his arsenal. "You drove me to my last doctor's appointment. You heard him tell me to take it easy."

Maddie joined Team Liam. "You'd be the boys' instructor. You don't have to go out on the river with them. Couldn't you instruct from the shoreline instead of in a canoe?"

Except that Aiden never stood on the shoreline. He used the clipboard to check off names, and the rest of the lesson took place on the river.

He flicked a look at the teenagers.

They needed a coach…and Aiden needed one more chance to get them to change their minds.

"All right, then. I'll let you get a look at the course first thing tomorrow morning. Come back at eight," Aiden said.

The expressions on the teenagers' faces were almost comical, but Tyler, naturally, was the first one to question their instructor.

"Why? Isn't it on the map?"

"Yes, it is." The map showed the river as a thin blue line with no current, downed trees or protruding rocks. Xs marked the obstacles but didn't show the rugged terrain around them. "But trust me. It isn't the same as seeing it up close."

"They'll be here," Maddie promised.

Aiden unleashed a slow smile. "And so will you."

"Me?"

"You said you needed a coach…" Aiden patted his knee. "And I need a driver."

Chapter Nine

"Wow."

Connie Donoghue, who occasionally filled in for Maddie at the library when she needed time off, almost dropped a copy of *Shakespeare's Greatest Works* on her foot when Maddie came around the corner.

"What's the matter?"

"Um… I don't think I've ever seen you wear that before."

Maddie plucked at the zipper of her jacket. "It's new." It was also a bright canary yellow, the only color on the rack in her size because she hadn't had time to order one online. "What do you think?"

"I didn't know there was a vintage fleece line."

Maddie narrowed her eyes. "Are you laughing at me?"

"Not until you walk out the door."

Maddie didn't take offense. Her outfit *was* an eclectic fusion of practical and thrift shop chic. A handmade fisherman's sweater, knit from yards of soft, cream-colored yarn. Slim tweed pants cuffed at the tops of a pair of hiking shoes she'd found on clearance at the same time she'd purchased the jacket.

She could only imagine Aiden's reaction when she arrived.

Aiden had had a diabolical gleam in his eye when he'd drafted her to be his driver. Come to think of it, the gleam had appeared when he'd suggested they take a look at the course.

What had she gotten them into?

No, what had she gotten *herself* into?

The plan had been to convince Aiden to take the teenagers under his wing, not serve as his wingman. Or, more accurately, his wing *girl*.

Maddie wasn't supposed to be part of this at all. She was supposed to be helping the teenagers prepare for their senior presentations at the library while Aiden prepared them for River Quest.

"Thanks for coming in on such short notice." Maddie grabbed her purse from the shelf behind the circulation desk. "And for locking up this afternoon."

"Unpacking a box of books is a tough way to spend a few hours," Connie teased. "But I'll take one for the team."

Maddie cast a longing glance at the cardboard box packed with new fiction. No matter how skilled the authors, the many twists and turns those stories would take weren't as unpredictable as the ones waiting outside the door.

Loud voices carried through the window.

And speaking of *team*…

Maddie had told the teenagers to meet her at the library if they needed a ride out to Aiden's, but she was surprised to see that Skye and Tyler had actually taken her up on the offer.

The teenagers stood a few feet apart on the sidewalk. The conversation they'd been having was clearly over, and they were scowling down at their cell phones instead of each other.

Back to square one.

When she stepped outside, the teenagers returned Maddie's greeting with a mumbled hello and climbed into the back seat of her car.

Maddie glanced at her watch. "I think we'll wait a few minutes to see if Justin shows up."

"He isn't coming."

"At all?"

"I don't know." Skye shrugged. "He didn't say."

Disappointment arrowed through her. Out of the three teens, there was something about Justin that tugged at Maddie's heart. The boy didn't say much, but she had a feeling he didn't miss a thing. Tyler was always connected to his phone, Skye to her notebook, but Justin…he always seemed to be on the outside looking in.

Oh, how Maddie could relate. She'd felt like the odd man out when she was that age, too.

Maddie's parents, who'd discouraged her from participating in any activities that would have put a strain on her heart, hadn't realized the strain that had put on her social life instead. Dances, slumber parties, school-sponsored events. Maddie had declined so many invitations her classmates had eventually stopped extending them. And in a high school where athletes were treated like small-town royalty, a girl who'd spent four years helping the school librarian shelve books had been practically invisible.

She waited until they were settled before she put the car in gear.

"How is everyone doing today?"

Tyler grunted, and she caught Skye's eye roll in the rearview mirror.

Okay, then.

"Did you—" Maddie's foot stomped the brake as someone darted into the street.

Justin.

Maddie pressed her hand against her heart to hold it in place as he scrambled into the back seat.

"I could have hit you!"

"Sorry," he mumbled, the word barely audible over the click of his seat belt.

Maddie glanced in the rearview mirror, but Justin wouldn't meet her eyes. She was tempted to ask if something was wrong, but she didn't want to put him on the spot in front of Tyler and Skye.

Lord, you know them. You know what they need. Show them how valuable they are in your eyes.

When they arrived, Aiden was already waiting for them outside. Instead of his usual flannel, he wore a windproof jacket with multiple pockets over a black T-shirt, and had switched out his jeans for loose-fitting Gore-Tex pants.

His gaze swept over the teenagers as they bailed out of the car before it settled on Maddie.

She lifted her chin. "I know. I know. I'm the color and shape of a marshmallow Peep."

"I'm not saying a word." Aiden's lips twitched, and he held up a key fob. "Let's go."

Maddie looked from Aiden to the mud-spattered side-by-side parked a few yards away. "You want me to drive *that*?"

"It handles like a four-wheeler..." Aiden stopped. "You've never driven a four-wheeler?"

Maddie shook her head. The only vehicles she'd driven came equipped with standard features. Like windows. And doors.

"Okay. Not a problem. Think of it as a Kia. With roll bars." Aiden paused. "And beastly tires."

"If you'd like, I can pull up a satellite image of the area on my laptop to see the course." Maddie didn't know why she hadn't thought of that before. "That way, we wouldn't take up as much of your time."

Aiden stared at Maddie as if she'd just offered to fly him to the moon.

No, *everyone* was staring at Maddie as if she'd offered to fly them to the moon.

"It's very accurate," she murmured.

The twitch Maddie had seen playing at the corners of Aiden's lips turned into a full-blown grin. "But not as much fun."

The expressions on the teenagers' faces told her they agreed with their guide.

And because Maddie was the team sponsor—and Aiden's designated driver—she sent up a silent prayer that she wouldn't make a complete fool of herself, then took the key from Aiden's hand.

"Hold on a second!" Sunni emerged from the house and bustled toward them, holding up a large insulated bag and a thermos. Her smile expanded to include the teenagers. "All this fresh air is guaranteed to make you hungry, so I thought you might need a midmorning snack."

It looked like Sunni had packed enough food to feed the entire senior class, but Maddie didn't hear any complaints.

"That was really nice of you, Mrs. Mason."

"I like to cook…and it's a good thing, because I had to feed three boys who liked to eat!" Sunni tucked the cooler and thermos into a separate compartment in the back of the utility vehicle. "It's a perfect day to be outside enjoying God's creation. The color is going to be beautiful for the fall festival this year." She gave Aiden's shoulder an affectionate pat. "I'll let you get on your way."

Sunni took a step backward, but Aiden caught hold of her arm. "Can you do one more thing for us, Mom?"

"Of course, sweetheart."

"Take care of the cell phones until we get back."

A chorus of groans instantly rose from the ranks.

"Why?" Tyler demanded.

"Where we're going is a dead zone." Aiden looked at Justin, and the boy's ears turned red.

"I don't have one," he muttered.

For a moment, Tyler looked as if he was going to refuse to comply with the request, and then he reluctantly turned it over.

Skye didn't look convinced. "What if there's an emergency?" she asked nervously.

Aiden grinned. "You'll get some great footage for your video?"

Skye laughed, but Sunni swatted his arm. "Aiden! Don't tease the poor girl!"

No, keep teasing her, Maddie thought. Because Skye's laughter sounded sweeter than the wind in the trees.

Did Aiden even realize that simply by being himself—his audacious, funny, adventurous self—he was giving the teenagers the freedom to be themselves, too?

"I'll take good care of them." Sunni sealed the promise with a wink as Skye, too, relinquished her phone.

"Thanks, Mom." Aiden turned to Maddie. "Ready when you are."

Suddenly, Maddie didn't feel ready at all.

She slid behind the wheel and waited for Aiden to climb in beside her. The dashboard didn't look anything like that of a compact car, but at least the gas pedal and the brake were in their proper places.

"Where are we going?"

"Just follow the trail."

Maddie didn't see a trail, but she put the UTV in gear and it shot forward like a bull released from a chute.

Her passengers, taking a page from Aiden's playbook, let out a cheer. As if Maddie had done it on purpose.

"I should have warned you. I tinkered with the engine a little," Aiden whispered. "To give it more snort."

He could have mentioned that a little earlier.

The vehicle began to crawl forward, and just when Maddie was starting to get the hang of it, Justin let out a yelp.

Considering the sound came from a boy who barely spoke above a whisper, Maddie reacted with a quick stomp on the brake.

Aiden slid sideways into the metal frame and groaned. “Are you kidding me?”

“I’m sorry!” Maddie’s gaze bounced from the cast on Aiden’s wrist to his injured knee as he tried to turn around in his seat.

“I wasn’t talking to you. I was talking to him.” Aiden pointed at the dog limping along behind them.

Without a word, Tyler jumped down, scooped Dodger up in his arms and deposited him in the back.

Dodger responded to the help by baring his teeth, and then promptly wedged himself in the space between Justin and Skye’s feet.

Maddie took that as her cue to continue on their journey.

This was Aiden’s world, not hers. But she felt a shiver of anticipation, wondering where it would take her.

Aiden usually felt more at home, more at peace, here in the woods than he did in his own living room.

But not today.

Today he felt frustrated and…guilty.

“According to the map—” Skye leaned over the seat “—one of the obstacles is pretty close.”

“Just around the corner,” Aiden said.

“Corner?” Maddie murmured.

“Just pretend that stump up ahead is a stop sign and hang a quick right.”

“I’ll turn right,” she said. “But I make no promises that it will be quick.”

Aiden grinned. It seemed the fresh air was stirring up a little spunk in his librarian.

No, not *his* librarian.

The librarian who’d agreed to help Aiden find his sister.

The librarian whose plan he still intended to sabotage.

Hence the guilt.

Aiden had said no refunds, but he planned to give her one anyway. If everything went the way he expected it would, the ink on the sponsorship form Maddie had signed would still be wet when they returned.

What was that old saying? The end justifies the means? In this case, Aiden decided, the means justified the end.

Which was why he'd confiscated their cell phones.

Aiden wanted the kids to feel uneasy. Realize they were out of their element. There were at least a dozen different ways that weekend warriors could get hurt if they didn't pay attention to their surroundings.

Maddie had said she wanted to build confidence in the teenagers, but wouldn't washing out of the competition after the first or second challenge be worse?

He was doing them a favor, right?

An image of Rich Mason's face suddenly flashed in his mind. His foster dad had instilled a love for the outdoors in Aiden, but he hadn't left it at that. Every time Rich had pointed to something in nature, whether it was a tuft of moss growing in the cleft of a rock or a bald eagle in flight, he'd reminded Aiden that everything in creation pointed to the Creator of the entire universe.

Rich hadn't simply talked about what he believed, though. He'd lived it.

Not only had Aiden's foster dad founded Castle Falls Outfitters around a passage in the Bible, he'd left a legacy of faith that Aiden wanted to pass on to his own family someday.

Just as soon as he found the right woman to start that family *with*.

In spite of Aiden's best efforts to keep his eyes trained on the trail ahead, his gaze edged back toward Maddie with the relentless pull of a needle on a compass seeking the North Pole.

The UTV bounced over a root that had erupted from the ground, and Maddie's grip on the steering wheel tightened. Dozens of cockleburs had already hitched a ride and burrowed into her fleece jacket, so deep she'd have to use patience and tweezers to get them out. Aiden knew better than to wear fleece on a trek into the woods, but at least in that particular shade of yellow, Maddie wouldn't get lost.

She was obviously out of her element, so maybe Aiden was doing her a favor, too.

The thought ran through his mind even as he battled a sudden urge to skip the scheduled tour and show Maddie all the places he loved to hang out. The rocks that formed a natural walkway over a narrow part of the river. The skeletal frame of a fallen oak that Aiden had pretended was a pirate ship when he was younger. The sunny spot on the riverbank where Ben and Jerry, two young otters, lazed away the afternoons.

Would Maddie see a wonderland to explore? Or a wilderness she would be eager to escape at the end of the day?

The second scenario was the most likely, and also the most convenient for him, considering his pretty driver's change of heart was the end game here.

Aiden ignored another stab of guilt, pushing it aside like he did the rest of his pain.

"The first land obstacle is called The Pendulum." Skye's voice was a jolting reminder there were three other passengers—four if you counted Dodger—in the vehicle. "What's that?"

"It's hard to describe." Aiden smiled as Maddie drove into an empty clearing.

"Where is it?" Tyler asked.

Funny. Aiden had just been wondering the same thing.

"I'm not sure." Even to his own ears, Aiden's voice

sounded as tight as his grip on the roll bar. "Maybe Bren and Liam built it closer to the river."

Maddie cut the engine. Skye and Tyler bailed out, but Justin scooped up Dodger and set him down on the ground.

Aiden pried his crutch out from between the seats so he could take a closer look. His gut tightened as he surveyed the area. A pile of lumber marked the spot where there should have been a wall, and a blue tarp protected Liam's tools from the weather.

The Fall Festival was less than a month away, and neither one of his brothers had mentioned they were behind schedule. In fact, whenever Aiden asked for an update on the course, they'd claimed things were "going fine."

Call him crazy, but in Aiden's mind, "fine" translated to "almost finished."

"Is something wrong?" Maddie stood at his side, her voice soft with concern.

"I thought my brothers would have it done by now." Aiden tried to cover his frustration with a no-big-deal shrug. "But they must have gotten busy with something else."

Maddie's gaze shifted away from him. She took a swift but thorough sweep of the clearing before her gaze came to rest on the stack of lumber. "What were they supposed to build?"

"There's going to be a platform there." Aiden pointed to a natural split in the thick branches halfway up a towering pine. "The first objective is to climb the tree, grab the rope on the platform and swing over the wall." The wall his brothers hadn't gotten around to building yet. "The second objective is to let go once you're on the other side."

Tyler and Justin tipped their heads back, their eyes widening in direct proportion to the height of the tree.

"We have to climb up there?" Tyler asked.

"Only one of you," Aiden said. "The other one stays in

the canoe and meets up with you at the next checkpoint. It's not too far…a quarter of a mile as the crows flies."

Without a word, Maddie pivoted and walked away.

This was it. The other teenagers would follow her lead, and Aiden could breathe a sigh of relief.

Except that Maddie wasn't walking toward the UTV… she was walking over to the lumber.

"We'd better get started, then."

"What are you doing?" Aiden was almost afraid to ask. Because Maddie wasn't supposed to be rallying people to get started. She was supposed to convince them to withdraw from the competition.

She blew a loose strand of hair off her forehead and smiled.

"Building you a wall."

"It's not that I don't appreciate the offer, Maddie," Aiden said slowly. "But it's not just hammering boards together. Liam was going to draw up a plan to make sure the person holding the rope sails over the wall instead of crashing into it. The angle between the platform and the wall has to be perfect, or someone could get hurt. The goal is to challenge people, not maim them."

"We could start it, though," Tyler said. "It can't be that hard to pound a few boards together."

Aiden's gaze moved to Justin, who was frowning up at the tree. *Yes.* Aiden had someone on his side.

"Justin?"

"I can figure out the angles so no one gets hurt."

"What?" *What?*

"He's a math geek," Tyler said.

Justin shrugged self-consciously. "I like numbers."

The boys turned toward Skye, who rolled her eyes.

"Sure. Why not? It's not like I have anything else to do on a Saturday."

If Aiden had heard so much as a hint of sarcasm in

Skye's tone, he would have pushed instead of giving up. Still, he felt obligated to try one more time.

"You really want to spend the day building a wall?"

It was Maddie who answered for the group. "The team has a vested interest in The Pendulum, don't we?"

Aiden laughed. At himself and at the best-laid plans.

"I guess you do."

Chapter Ten

Four hours later, Maddie had a much quieter group than she'd had when they'd left earlier that morning.

Aiden was pretty quiet, too, although his fingers tapped out an uneven beat against his knee.

Maddie had been just as surprised as Aiden when she'd suggested—no, informed him—they would build the wall. And she hadn't understood his initial reluctance any more than she'd been able to decipher the rueful smile that had tipped Aiden's lips when he'd finally agreed.

The kids had made Maddie proud, though, from the beginning of the project to the moment they'd trudged back to the UTV together, damp and coated in sawdust.

It was the *together* part that had had Maddie sending up a silent cheer.

"There you are!" Brendan's wife was waiting for them when Maddie pulled up next to the garage. Lily, a marketing whiz who'd lived in an urban area before making Castle Falls her permanent home, appeared to be completely at home in her new surroundings. "I was about to send out a search party!"

"A search party?" Aiden repeated. "I knew my oldest brother would be a bad influence on you."

"Your oldest brother happens to be perfect. And yes, a

little overprotective, but he's working on that." Lily flashed a warm smile at Maddie, the one that had instantly won the hearts of everyone in their small town, as well as Brendan Kane's. "Do you and Aiden need help putting things away?"

You and Aiden.

The words lit on Maddie's heart, stirring up a whole myriad of strange emotions. But it was too dangerous to allow them to linger there.

"Thanks, but my crew has it covered," Aiden told his sister-in-law.

Amazingly enough, the members of his "crew" didn't protest.

"So…how did it go?" Lily turned to the teenagers. "Was the course what you expected?"

"Nope," Tyler mumbled around the sugar cookie he'd popped into his mouth before handing the container to Maddie. "We didn't get to see it."

"You were gone for almost three hours." Lily looked like she didn't know whether to laugh or express concern. "Did the UTV break down again?"

Again?

Maddie looked at Aiden, whose attention had shifted to the tufts of clouds drifting over their heads.

"We finished The Pendulum instead." Tyler gave Justin a shoulder bump that sent the other boy stumbling sideways. "And the next time we come over, Justin here is going to test it out and make sure it works."

"It'll work."

To Maddie's absolute delight, Justin found his footing and shoulder-bumped Tyler right back.

"If the next time is tomorrow, you'll have to join us for supper afterward." Lily smiled at Maddie. "Our Sunday tradition is homemade pizza, and Sunni always makes enough food to feed a small army."

"I—" Maddie bit her lip. "I wasn't planning to come back. Aiden—"

"Has a bum knee, two cracked ribs and only one hand that works," he interjected smoothly. "So like it or not, you're part of the team now."

The glint in Aiden's eyes had returned, reminding Maddie that the "team" had been her idea.

But the trouble was, Maddie *did* like the idea. Too much. She'd imagined Aiden would take over from here, and she would receive updates from the teens when they met with her at the library. Once again, though, Aiden had changed the plan.

"The library is closed on Sundays, right?" Skye must have sensed Maddie's hesitation. And the fact that the girl looked nervous at the thought of joining Aiden's family for dinner tipped the balance in Lily's favor. She didn't want Skye to feel uncomfortable.

"Yes." Maddie nibbled on her lower lip. "I suppose I could."

"Great." Lily's violet eyes sparkled. "I'll tell Sunni to expect four more for pizza tomorrow night. Now, I'd better scoot or Brendan will send out a search party for *me*. I've been waiting for the delivery truck to drop off some light fixtures that Liam ordered, and I want to take them out to the cabin before he gets back."

"Back from where?" Aiden's eyebrows dipped together in a frown. "Aren't he and Bren working on the cabin this afternoon?"

Lily shook her head. "A water pipe broke at the animal shelter while you were gone. They went over to fix it, and I plan to grab a mop and help Sunni when I get back."

"It will take you a good half an hour to drive out to the cabin and back." A muscle tightened in Aiden's jaw, and Maddie instantly understood why.

As much as he wanted to, Aiden couldn't help his brothers with that project, either.

"I can take the lights over to the cabin." Maddie shocked herself—and Aiden, judging from the look on his face—for the second time that day. "If you don't mind dropping Tyler and Justin and Skye off on your way through town."

"Not at all." Lily's eyes lit up. "That would be wonderful! Aiden knows the way."

"Oh, but I..." Maddie cut a sideways glance at the man standing next to her. "Aiden doesn't have to come along. He can just point me in the right direction."

"It would be easier to show you," Lily said cheerfully. "Unless Aiden is getting tired—"

"Aiden," he interrupted, "is standing right here, listening to every word you're saying, and he's fine."

That seemed to settle the matter.

Maddie helped Lily load up the shipping boxes while Aiden and Dodger waited in the UTV.

"Being outside today has been good for him," Lily murmured. "He needed some fresh air and sunshine."

"Still here...and I'm not one of Mom's houseplants."

Lily winked at Maddie, which made her like the woman even more. "Thanks again for doing this. I'll see you tomorrow afternoon."

Maddie hopped into the driver's seat again after they left, buckled her seat belt and looked at her navigator for instructions.

"Go that way." Aiden pointed to a well-worn path winding into the woods in the opposite direction of the one they'd taken earlier that morning. And this one was easier to follow because it actually *looked* like a trail.

"Liam is building a cabin?"

Aiden nodded. "He and Anna and the twins will be moving into it after they're married. He had to expand the original plan, though, because it was only big enough for one person."

"When is the wedding?"

"Christmas Eve."

Maddie was thrilled for Anna, but that didn't prevent a tiny curl of envy from forming in the pit of her stomach. Any dreams she'd had of her future wedding day had been carefully tucked away the day Maddie discovered that children wouldn't be part of that future.

"I'm sure they're going to love living there," she said softly.

"Liam's behind schedule, though. Brendan and I were helping with the project, and now they have to help *me* finish the course for River Quest."

"I'm sure they don't mind," Maddie murmured. "And you'd do the same for them, if the situation was reversed, wouldn't you?"

Aiden responded with a clipped nod. "Of course. But it's different."

"How..." Maddie stopped when Aiden's breath hissed between his teeth.

The UTV hadn't hit another bump, but Maddie lifted her foot off the gas and turned toward him, certain he'd somehow reinjured his arm or his knee.

Aiden wasn't looking at her at all. Maddie followed his gaze and saw a pickup truck—or rather what was left of one—crouched in the shadows of an old shed no more than fifty yards into the woods. Shards of twisted metal spiraled from the hood, and fragments of shattered glass outlined the gaping hole where the driver's-side window had been.

The world seemed to shift, and two thoughts collided in Maddie's mind.

This was the truck Aiden had been driving the night of the accident.

And it was clearly only by the grace of God that he'd survived.

* * *

Aiden couldn't take his eyes off the chunk of scrap metal that had once been his pickup truck.

No wonder his brothers hadn't told him it was here. They must have towed it into the woods under cover of darkness in order to spare Aiden from seeing something that would remind him of the accident.

As if the cast on his arm and a messed-up knee weren't enough of a reminder as to how quickly things had gone south on Razor Road that night.

Its official name was Razorback, but the locals had shortened the name to Razor because that's what it looked like. A smooth, three-mile stretch of road that took a sharp turn a few miles from town. Even in good weather, people gave it the respect it deserved. Aiden always had, too, until someone had forced him to take a shortcut through the ditch.

Aiden tried to tear his gaze away, but seeing the truck triggered a tide of memories, and it was impossible to stop the flow.

The split-second decision Aiden had made began to play out again…only this time in slow motion.

The crunch of the tires against gravel as the truck slid off the road. The sensation of being airborne. The crushing jolt as the vehicle slammed against the ground before rolling once. Twice. The frame had crumpled as if it had had no more substance than a soda can. Stinging fragments of glass from the windshield raining down on him like sleet.

He'd struggled to keep his eyes open, but the darkness had crashed over him like a wave and swallowed him whole…

A featherlight touch brought him back to reality.

Maddie had taken his hand.

He tore his gaze away from the truck and experienced the sensation of falling all over again when he found himself staring into Maddie's green eyes. She let go, but Aiden could still feel the warm imprint of her fingers against his skin.

And even though she hadn't witnessed the crash, Aiden couldn't help but notice that she looked a little pale, too.

"Praise God," she whispered.

Aiden knew what Maddie meant. The truck was totaled, but he was alive. But right now, anger at the coward who'd left him in the ditch burned hotter than gratitude. Or forgiveness.

"I didn't know the truck was here." He pasted on a smile. "I shouldn't be surprised, though. My brothers have a habit of keeping things from me."

"Or they wanted to protect you from reliving the accident," Maddie said softly.

That word. *Accident.* Something inside Aiden broke loose, and the truth spilled out.

"I know what people are saying, but I wasn't speeding that night. Someone else was, and when he crossed the center line, I had to take the ditch to avoid a head-on collision." Aiden's gaze locked on the crumpled remains of his pickup again. "Whoever was driving forced me off the road and kept going."

As soon as he said the words, Aiden wished he could take them back, but he didn't want Maddie to join the long list of people who thought he was trying to cover his lapse in judgment with a lie.

"Aiden—"

"Never mind." He couldn't look at her. It was bad enough he'd seen the doubt in his brothers' eyes. Aiden couldn't bear to see it in Maddie's, too. "It's not like I can prove it."

Bitterness saturated his words, and Maddie realized the damage to Aiden's truck didn't begin to compare to the internal injuries he'd suffered.

Maddie stared at Aiden's pickup and tried to imagine who would have done what he'd claimed. Someone under the influence of drugs or alcohol? Or someone who'd been distracted one moment and terrified the next, when Aiden's truck had skidded into the ditch?

Either way, the driver should have stopped to help.

Lord, give me wisdom.

And just like that, the answer came to Maddie.

Let him tell his story.

"What happened?"

Aiden remained silent for so long, Maddie wasn't even sure he'd heard her ask the question.

"I don't remember." Aiden laughed, but there was no humor in it. "Now, that makes my claim sound legitimate, doesn't it?"

"You remember *something*," Maddie said evenly. "Or you wouldn't have told me there was another car."

The accident had made the local newspaper, but the article didn't say anything about another vehicle involved. Still, Maddie couldn't imagine Aiden making something like that up.

She'd heard people describe him as reckless, but it didn't fit the man who'd put the safety of the River Quest competitors first when he'd supervised the building of the wall that afternoon. Aiden might push the limits, but he didn't ignore them or pretend they weren't there just for an adrenaline rush.

"It was a truck," Aiden muttered. "The high beams blinded me for a second when it came around the corner. It all happened so fast. I thought we were going to hit head-on, so I took the ditch…and the truck kept going. I read Deputy Bristow's report and found out another driver called 911. He stayed with me until the rescue squad showed up."

Maddie had never met the deputy in person, but she

recognized the last name. Carter Bristow had sent in a registration form so his five-year-old daughter, Isabella, could attend the children's story hour Maddie hosted at the library, but the little girl's grandmother had always accompanied her.

"Is Deputy Bristow looking into it?"

"As far as I know, he closed the investigation because he couldn't find any evidence to back up what I said." Aiden's gaze slid to the truck again. "And according to my brothers, if you end up with a mild concussion, your memory isn't all that credible, either."

The shadows in Aiden's eyes had returned. Did he think Brendan and Liam doubted his story, too? If so, Maddie knew it would only add more weight to the burden he carried.

"What I *do* know is that someone wrecked my truck and my chance to..." His lips pressed together in a thin line, sealing off the words he'd been about to say. "Whoever it was should be held accountable. I'm not sure how, but I'm going to find out what happened."

Maddie wasn't sure what Aiden had been about to say, but she believed him. Judging from his expression, he was as committed to finding the person who'd run him off the road as he was to finding his sister.

She could only pray the truth that Aiden uncovered—in both of the searches—wouldn't bring more pain.

Chapter Eleven

Aiden heard the heavy tread of footsteps outside the door of the sunroom and closed his eyes.

"Aiden—"

"Shh." Liam's voice. "He's asleep."

"No, he's not. He's faking because he doesn't want to talk to us." The footsteps drew closer and stopped next to the couch. "You're awake, aren't you?"

"No."

"What did I tell you?"

Aiden cracked open one eye and saw his oldest brother grinning down at him.

"Dodger…attack."

The dog, camped out underneath the rocking chair, didn't so much as flash an incisor.

"Really? Selective snarling?" Aiden scowled at his roommate. "No more rawhide chews for you."

Brendan flopped into the chair across from Aiden. "So, what do you think of the obstacle course so far? Mom said you took a group of teenagers out there today."

I think it's not getting done as fast as you told me it would.

Aiden didn't dare voice the thought out loud, though. It was almost the end of September, but for the first time in a long time, business at Castle Falls Outfitters hadn't shown any signs of slowing down. His brothers already crammed more hours in during their workweek than most people. Aiden wasn't about to criticize them for not spending what little free time they had on a project that had been his idea in the first place.

He wasn't going to bring up the truck, either. In order to keep a grip on his emotions, Aiden had been trying to put it out of his mind…along with the memory of Maddie's touch.

A touch so light it shouldn't even have registered, and yet the effects had lingered the rest of the afternoon.

Brendan cleared his throat, and Aiden realized his brother was still waiting for an answer.

"What we saw looked good," Aiden said. "They didn't see the whole course."

"Why not?" Liam claimed the other empty chair. "Did you convince them to give up? Don't look at me like that, bro. I figured out your devious plan when we were in the Trading Post yesterday."

The plan that had backfired. Spectacularly. Maddie's students had worked tirelessly for four hours. But instead of giving up, the more they worked, the more excited they seemed to get about the competition.

Brendan frowned. "Why would he do that? I thought the goal was to register the maximum number of teams for the event."

"They need a little coaching, and Aiden claims it's a conflict of interest," Liam explained.

"It is," Aiden muttered.

Laughter gleamed in Liam's eyes. "I think you're conflicted about your interest, all right."

Aiden pushed into a sitting position. A guy couldn't effectively spar with his brothers while horizontal. "What is that supposed to mean?"

"It means I've seen Maddie Montgomery twice in the past twenty-four hours," Liam said. "And according to my sources, you've visited the local library a few times, too."

"Your sources?" Aiden repeated. "I want names."

"Don't change the subject." Brendan leaned back in the chair, crossed his arms behind his head. "This is getting interesting."

There was no way around it. Aiden was going to have to tell the truth. Or at least part of the truth. He could define his relationship with Maddie much easier than he could define all the conflicting emotions that relationship had brought into play.

"I've been at the library because Maddie agreed to help me."

"Help you what?" Liam bent down, reached under the chair and ruffled one of Dodger's ragged ears. "Are you finally going to finish that book report for freshman English?"

"I asked Maddie to help me find our sister."

Eyes rounded. Mouths dropped open. As if Aiden's statement had sucked all the oxygen from the room.

"The day Liam announced his engagement to Anna, I promised I would track her down before the wedding," he reminded them.

"I know." Brendan paused. "But Aiden…"

Based on past experience, Aiden knew those two words never preceded good news.

"What?" he demanded. "Isn't that the reason you told us? I was under the impression you *wanted* to find her."

Brendan flicked a look at Liam. "Of course we do."

That sounded convincing.

Did they think Aiden was going to mess this up, too?

Liam reached across the coffee table and gave Aiden's shoulder an encouraging little cuff. Aiden supposed he should be grateful his brother hadn't tried to scratch his ears, too.

"Bren's telling you the truth, Aiden, but we're just not sure…what if she doesn't want to be found?"

It had never occurred to Aiden their sister might be content with her life. That she might know she had siblings without feeling the need to *get* to know them.

"I have to try," Aiden said tightly.

Brendan and Liam exchanged The Look. They thought he was being stubborn. Or, even worse, that the search for their sister was simply one more challenge Aiden wanted to take on.

Fine. Better his brothers think there were reasons for the quest other than the guilt that had started to gnaw away at Aiden ever since Brendan had broken the news about their youngest sibling.

"You really think Maddie can track her down?" Liam waded bravely into the tense silence that had descended on the room. "It was a closed adoption. Wouldn't the records be sealed?"

"I'm not sure." Unfortunately, that thought *had* crossed Aiden's mind. Unlike him, Maddie wasn't very good at hiding her emotions. The moment Aiden had uttered the words "closed adoption," he'd seen the flicker of concern in her eyes. "But anything else Brendan can remember about the conversation between Carla and the social worker would be helpful."

"I told you everything I know." Brendan closed his eyes for a moment, as if he were trying to re-create a picture in his mind. "I'd skipped school that day because I couldn't stay awake in class. We'd spent half the night in the ER while the doctor stitched up your head after you fell off the fence at the park. I overheard Mom talking to someone in the kitchen and caught enough of the conversation to figure out what was going on. I couldn't confront her without admitting I'd been listening in, though, and I didn't want to get in trouble."

Aiden remembered the park, although it was a stretch to call it that. The square of concrete, once a small playground for a private school that had relocated to a safer part of the city, had become a gathering place for kids like Aiden and his brothers, who didn't want to be at home.

Aiden had a vague memory of grappling with a rusty chain-link fence because he'd decided it looked more fun than the swings. But it was a memory he shouldn't have had at all, if Brendan had gotten the details right.

"When you told us about our sister, you said I was about three at the time."

"Yeah. You were."

"I'm pretty sure I fell off that fence when I was five."

"No."

"He's right, Bren," Liam said. "The nurse said Aiden needed five stitches, and I remember him saying he knew how many that was because he was five years old."

Brendan still didn't look completely convinced. "So what happened when he was three?"

"That was the shopping cart debacle."

Aiden liked the way Liam summed things up. *Debacle* sounded so much better than "Aiden found an abandoned shopping cart, climbed inside and then proceeded to crash into the stop sign at the bottom of the hill."

"Right." Brendan shuddered at the memory. "I can't believe I blocked that one out."

"It's not your fault." Liam chucked a pillow at their brother. "It's Aiden's for ending up in the emergency room so many times."

Aiden knew his brother was trying to lighten the moment, but he didn't argue.

A lot of things that had happened in their family were his fault.

* * *

"Checkmate."

Maddie blinked and the chessboard came back into view. So did her dad's smiling face across the coffee table, and the king he'd neatly pinned in the corner with nothing more than a pawn and a rook.

"You won." Maddie couldn't even recall the move that had sealed the white kingdom's doom.

Ever since she'd arrived at her parents' house for their weekly Saturday night dinner, Maddie hadn't been able to prevent her wayward thoughts from straying beyond the walls of the living room.

Ordinarily, she looked forward to playing chess with her dad and sharing what had happened over the course of the week, but no matter how hard Maddie tried, the last conversation she'd had with Aiden kept scrolling through her mind.

"I certainly did," her dad agreed with a wink. He slid Maddie's king across the board. "Care for a rematch?"

"It's going to have to wait until after dessert." Tara Montgomery poked her head out of the kitchen. "Dinner is almost ready."

"I'll set the table while Dad basks in the glow of victory." Maddie rose to her feet and padded into the kitchen, where her mother was garnishing the salads with chunks of crusty bread and a dusting of Parmesan cheese.

Tara loved to cook, and meals had always been on the formal side while Maddie was growing up. Tonight, French onion soup simmered in a pot on the back of the stove, and steam rose from the rosemary chicken and red potatoes arranged on a platter.

A few hours ago, Maddie had been sitting cross-legged on the ground with her students, dipping tortilla chips in the bowl of fresh salsa Sunni had packed in the cooler and passing it around the circle while Aiden recounted some of his adventures to an exhausted but captivated work crew.

Maddie had been a little captivated, too.

Listening to Aiden, Maddie had witnessed the fun-loving daredevil who'd led countless expeditions into the wilderness. No wonder people requested him as their guide. Aiden could make anyone believe that things like lightning strikes and snakes napping under the seat in the canoe were all part of the outdoor experience.

Like any gifted storyteller, Aiden probably embellished the details a little—but Maddie had no doubt he'd been telling her the truth about the accident.

She'd left several hours ago, but the image of the crumpled pickup truck remained etched in Maddie's mind. Until now, she'd been able to separate Aiden's injuries from the accident that had caused them. Not anymore. Now she could match the damage—the shards of broken glass, the gouges and dents where the vehicle had connected with the ground—to the damage Aiden's body had sustained.

Maddie closed her eyes and thanked God again for sparing him.

"Maddie?" Her mom's voice broke through her thoughts. "Are you feeling all right?"

The picture dissolved, and Maddie realized she had one hand pressed against her middle.

It had to be hardwired in every mom, the ability to morph from gourmet chef to doctor in less than an instant. Tara abandoned the French silk pie on the counter and zoomed in for a closer look.

"I'm—" Maddie forced down the bile that had risen in her throat, a side effect that came from imagining a world without Aiden Kane "—fine, Mom."

Tara didn't look convinced. "You seem a little distracted today, sweetheart…and you look a little flushed. Are you sure?"

"Really, Mom." Maddie forced a smile. "I spent the afternoon outside, and my ten-hour sunscreen only lasted four."

"You should have called your dad if you needed help raking leaves. You know how much he enjoys puttering around outside."

Actually, Maddie knew that her dad, a retired high school history teacher, preferred to spend a Saturday afternoon in his study with a cup of French roast coffee and a Winston Churchill biography. He only "puttered around outside" when absolutely necessary. And he spent more time tending the postage-stamp-size lawn around the library than his own, so that Maddie wouldn't have to.

"I wasn't raking leaves today. The high school students I've been tutoring signed up for River Quest, so we checked out the course together." She decided not to mention they'd also helped *build* one of the obstacles for that course.

"On a Saturday?" Tara didn't look happy. "I thought you only met with your high school students during the week. And why are you chaperoning their field trips? Isn't that the school's responsibility?"

Maddie braced herself for another conversation about boundaries. If it were up to her parents, her duties at the library would cease when she locked the door at the end of the day.

"It's my responsibility because it was my idea. I got permission from the library board to sponsor the team." Maddie opened a drawer in the built-in china cabinet and retrieved three linen napkins embroidered with autumn leaves. "Last week I couldn't get the kids excited about anything, and now they can't wait to go back to Sunni Mason's tomorrow."

The frown that creased her mom's forehead told Maddie that her dad had mentioned seeing Aiden in the library. And that Tara had instantly connected the family dots.

"I read the article in the newspaper. Isn't Aiden Kane in charge of the event?"

"Mmm-hmm." Maddie edged toward the dining room, but her mom blocked her path, a sign the conversation wasn't over. "River Quest was Aiden's idea, but his whole family is involved."

"And he recruited your students?"

A smile surfaced before Maddie could prevent it. "Actually, it was the other way around. I recruited *him*. Justin and Tyler needed a coach."

"I understand your wanting to sponsor a team, sweetheart, but why can't you just write a check?"

Maddie could have...but she wouldn't have seen Justin and Tyler's looks of pride when they'd finished the wall. Wouldn't have heard Skye laugh.

Wouldn't have discovered the truth about Aiden's accident and seen a very different side to Castle Falls' most popular daredevil.

There'd been anger simmering in Aiden's eyes, but Maddie had been touched by the flash of vulnerability she'd seen, too. And it was the vulnerability that had had Maddie boldly reaching for his hand.

Aiden was light and shadow, as complex as the play of sunshine through the trees.

He was also fascinating. And handsome...

"Maddie..." Tara paused, and Maddie knew what was coming next. "Please promise me that you won't do anything that puts your heart at risk."

"I won't."

But even as she said the words, Maddie worried it might already be too late.

Chapter Twelve

"Which one do you like the best, Miss M?"

Maddie, whose job description included reminding people to keep their voices down, wanted to shout for joy when Skye slid her notebook across the picnic blanket.

It would have been the third time that afternoon.

The weather was perfect again—golden sunshine laced with a pine-scented breeze that barely ruffled the surface of the river.

Shortly after they'd arrived on Sunday afternoon, Aiden had gone through the list of safety instructions with the two boys and called out tips as they launched the canoe.

Skye had been alternately recording the boys' progress and sketching in the ever-present notebook, but Maddie hadn't realized the girl was working on ideas for the team flag.

A yelp and a splash drew her attention back to the boys. The canoe was rocking back and forth as Tyler attempted to retrieve his ball cap from the river.

"If I can't turn this into a senior project, at least I can use it for blackmail," Skye joked.

"I like this one." Maddie pointed to Skye's drawing of a comet, its tail separating into ribbons of crimson and orange flames. "It fits your team name."

The Flamethrowers had been Tyler's top pick for a name, and the others, of course, had gone along with it.

"And the canoe," Skye said.

Right. The canoe. Maddie hid a wince. When Aiden had told the boys to grab one of the canoes, he hadn't quite been able to hide his look of dismay when they'd returned a few minutes later carrying a canoe emblazoned with crimson flames that flowed from bow to stern.

It wasn't part of the fleet that Castle Falls rented for excursions on the river, Maddie realized. It was Aiden's canoe, his personal property, but the only thing he'd said was, "Good choice."

"That one is my favorite, too…but do you think they'll like it?" Skye scratched at the turquoise polish on her thumbnail.

At the beginning of their meetings, Skye had squared off against Tyler like opposing boxers in a ring and ignored Justin completely. Now she seemed almost anxious for their approval.

Maddie had been hoping that River Quest would boost the teenagers' confidence, but the tentative friendship she could see forming wasn't just an added bonus—it was a blessing.

She shaded her eyes against the sun and watched the boys as they tried to maneuver the canoe through the rocks that jutted from the surface of the water like tiny islands. Aiden timed them from the riverbank, stopwatch in hand, standing next to the Adirondack chair Liam had planted in the grass instead of relaxing in it.

Maddie had seen Aiden absently rub his rib cage or brace his hand against a tree while he coached Tyler and Justin. There'd also been times Aiden had glanced at one of the empty canoes on shore and Maddie was sure he was going to disregard the doctor's orders and sail off down the river after them.

Maddie hadn't quite known what to expect today, but Aiden's restless energy didn't translate into impatience or flashes of temper. He was a natural teacher, balancing encouragement and constructive criticism with the same skill he used to wield the ever-present aluminum crutch.

Maddie had a feeling that Aiden was harder on himself than he was on other people.

"They made it through this time!" Skye vaulted to her feet. "Come on!"

Maddie followed the girl down to the river and waited for the boys to return to shore.

"You shaved off twenty seconds." Aiden slipped the stopwatch into the front pocket of his jeans. "You made some progress, so I think we're at a good place to stop for the day. Time to recharge with a pepperoni pizza."

Tyler and Justin actually looked disappointed.

Maddie considered that a blessing, too.

"Can we come back tomorrow?" Tyler unclipped the buckles on his life jacket. "We're ready for The Cauldron, aren't we, Justin?"

The other boy bobbed his head while Maddie suppressed the urge to shake hers.

The Cauldron. The Pendulum. The Serpent's Tail.

Some of the challenges required physical strength and some relied on speed or navigational skill, but Maddie had a sneaking suspicion the man who'd designed the course had also been the one responsible for giving every obstacle a name designed to heighten the suspense surrounding the competition.

"Don't you have school tomorrow?" Aiden pointed his finger and drew an invisible arch from the dripping life jacket in Tyler's hand to a hook protruding from the side of a small shed.

Maddie watched in amazement as the boy responded

to the unspoken command without a word of complaint. "Not if you let us come back."

"I'll tell you what. You can come back next Friday if the librarian gives you a free pass from your study session."

Three hopeful pairs of eyes swung toward Maddie.

"We could do that…if everyone turns in their topic and an outline when we meet tomorrow night."

Maddie heard grumbles as the teenagers charged up the riverbank, but at least it no longer sounded like they were planning a mutiny.

Aiden fell silent as he and Maddie followed at a slower pace. In spite of the injury to his knee, Aiden moved with an athlete's natural grace, but there was no hiding the fact he was still in pain.

The tip of the crutch hit a patch of soft ground, and when Maddie reached out to prevent him from falling, she instantly had a flashback to the morning Aiden had come into the library. Only this time, instead of glaring at her, he tucked her arm more securely in the crook of his elbow.

Steadying himself while Maddie felt curiously *unsteady.*

Not. Good.

"I… I don't think I'm going to be able to join you for supper after all," she stammered, easing her hand free. "The kids drove together, so they can stay. The library is having a used book sale during the fall festival, and the drop box outside the library is usually overflowing by the end of the weekend."

Aiden tilted his head toward the sky. "It's twenty after four…technically, there's a few hours left before the end of the weekend."

Maddie couldn't stop herself from glancing at her wristwatch.

Four twenty on the dot.

"How did you *do* that?"

"I'll tell you if you change your mind and stay for

pizza." Aiden grinned down at her. "My family can be a little noisy, but they're not nearly as scary as Dodger here."

Maddie wasn't scared of the dog. She'd quickly figured out that Dodger's snaps and snarls were strictly for show.

No, it was the side effects she experienced from one of Aiden's grins that were downright dangerous.

Aiden might not have been able to personally take on any of the challenges today, but when Maddie nodded, it felt like he'd won a victory.

Instead of following the teenagers into the house, Aiden veered toward the spacious cedar deck that stretched the length of the sunroom. He'd been telling the truth when he'd told Maddie his family wasn't scary, but that didn't mean they couldn't be a little overwhelming when they were all together in the same room.

"You have a beautiful view." Maddie perched on one of the Adirondack chairs.

Aiden hadn't sat outside on the deck or admired the view for days, but watching the river flow past without him didn't stir feelings of resentment anymore.

Maybe because he'd been so focused on making sure Tyler and Justin didn't capsize his canoe, there hadn't been time to dwell on the fact that Aiden wasn't the one paddling it.

Or maybe it was because he was enjoying *this* view. Instead of tracing the curve of the river, Aiden found himself drawn to Maddie's profile as she lifted her face toward the sky. Gold-tipped lashes almost brushed the lenses on her glasses, and three tiny amber dots, a lone constellation separated from the shower of freckles across her nose, marked her cheekbone.

"Ahem."

Brendan—and Maddie's students—had somehow sneaked onto the deck without Aiden noticing them.

"Where did you come from?"

"The sliding glass doors behind you." Brendan could barely contain his smirk. "I'd tell you to have your hearing checked, but it was pretty obvious your attention was on…other things."

Aiden wasn't going to deal with his brother's know-it-all attitude right now. He'd wait until there were no witnesses.

Skye skirted the boys and landed in front of Maddie. "Miss M, can we go on another field trip?" she asked eagerly. "To the cave behind the waterfall?"

"Sunni just kicked us out of the kitchen, so I can lead the expedition," Brendan explained. "We'll be back in time for supper."

Maddie didn't answer right away.

"They won't get lost, Maddie," Aiden joked, not wanting her to see how frustrating it was that he couldn't be the one to explore the cave with Skye and the boys. "I taught my big brother everything I know."

"All right," Maddie finally said. "But stay with Brendan. No going off on your own."

The three teenagers responded to her warning with vigorous nods of agreement, and then the ragtag, sunburned explorers fell into line behind Brendan and disappeared into the woods.

"Don't worry. Brendan will keep an eye on them," Aiden said, sensing Maddie's concern.

She was the one responsible for the teenagers, so it was understandable she'd be concerned for their safety. The quick, uncertain look Maddie cut in his direction, though, told Aiden that her concern was for *him*.

Because he couldn't go along.

They'd barely spent any time together. How was it that Maddie was able to read his thoughts as easily as Aiden could read the sun's position in the sky?

"Uncle Aiden!"

Aiden braced himself for impact as Anna's twins

rounded the corner of the house, copper braids flying out behind them. He was new to the whole uncle thing, but it was pretty hard to resist an engaging grin and a freckled face. Especially in duplicate form.

"How did you find me?"

Chloe pointed to the couple holding hands as they walked down to the river. "Mom and Dad."

It wasn't the first time Aiden had heard the girls refer to Liam that way, but it still sparked a tickly feeling in the back of his throat. His brother had made the transition from die-hard bachelor to dad appear as effortless as a stroll in the park.

"Spies everywhere." Aiden hooked his good arm around his niece's waist and tickled her ribs until she broke free with a giggle.

"Miss Maddie!"

Aiden was instantly forgotten when Cassie spotted the woman sitting in the chair on the other side of the deck. She charged toward Maddie. Chloe, who tended to be the more cautious of the dynamic duo, was right at her heels. "I got an A on my book report last week!"

"I had a feeling you would." Maddie reached out and gave Cassie's braid a playful tug. "The illustrations you added were wonderful."

Aiden looked at the cozy little circle. "I take it you three know each other?"

The twins whirled toward him. Two pairs of golden-brown eyes rounded in disbelief.

"Miss Maddie is the *librarian*, Uncle Aiden," Chloe said, as if that explained everything.

"Cassie and Chloe drop by the library a few times a week." Maddie smiled. "They're the ones who inspired me to invite the author of the Winter series to visit the library during the Bountiful Books event in November."

"Who is Winter?" Aiden asked.

"A snowy owl." Maddie smiled at the girls. "He's the main character in a series for young readers."

"I'll show you, Uncle Aiden!" Cassie disappeared into the sunroom and returned a few minutes later, book in hand.

"The author is an award-winning pastel artist, too. She does all the illustrations for the series." Maddie bent closer to the twins as Aiden paged through it. "In fact, the newest one just came in the mail a few days ago. Would you like me to set it aside for you? I'll tell your mom that she can stop by and pick it up tomorrow."

"Yes!" Cassie and Chloe slapped their hands together in an enthusiastic high five.

"I haven't read the books, but I think Winter and I might have met in person." Aiden pulled up a picture on his phone, and Cassie squealed again.

"It's him!" She grabbed Maddie's hand and tugged her closer. "Look, Miss Maddie."

"You took this?"

"Uh-huh." Aiden grinned. "He's a regular. Stops by on his migration north and spends a few nights in his favorite tree. I can show you where it is, if you're interested. A picture in a book doesn't compare to seeing it up close."

Instead of looking excited by the opportunity, Maddie's expression clouded.

While Aiden was trying to figure out what he'd said and, more important, how he was going to fix it, Sunni, Lily and Anna came out to the deck carrying trays of homemade pizza.

His sister-in-law's statement that Sunni enjoyed having people join them for dinner hadn't been quite accurate. Aiden had been present when Lily broke the news, and Sunni had looked downright thrilled. Especially when she'd heard Maddie's name on the guest list.

"I hope you're all hungry!" Lily sang out.

Aiden handed the book back to Chloe and patted his abdomen. "Starving."

It was the only word he had a chance to say over the next two hours. When Cassie and Chloe weren't chattering about their upcoming adventures with the Sunflowers, a weekly kids club sponsored by New Life Fellowship, Aiden's older brothers entertained Maddie's students with stories about their move from the city to the pristine wilderness of the Upper Peninsula.

While they relayed humorous details about their encounters with nature—including an unexpected meeting with a cranky skunk—Aiden couldn't help but notice Brendan and Liam left out the details of what had preceded the move to Castle Falls. Like the fact that even though their mother had lived in the same house, she'd never made it a home.

How many times during the first ten years of Aiden's life had Brendan taken over for their parents? Made sure he and Liam got to school on time? Paid a visit to the neighborhood food pantry when the fridge was bare? And Liam—he'd been the classic middle child. The peacekeeper who could defuse a potentially volatile situation with a word or a look.

Aiden, on the other hand, had either been smack dab in the center of those volatile situations or, from the accusations their mother had thrown at him, the match that had ignited them.

Brendan and Liam might have forgotten who'd caused most of the discord in their family, but Aiden hadn't. He couldn't change the past, but it wasn't too late to make up for some of his mistakes now...and maybe change the way his brothers treated him in the future.

"Someone should be writing down all these stories." Anna nudged Liam. "For future generations to enjoy."

A dreamy look came over Sunni's face, and Aiden could almost *see* visions of copper-haired, blue-eyed grandchildren dancing in her head.

"Like we do in our Sunflower journals!" The twins had plopped down on either side of Maddie like bookends, and Cassie surreptitiously deposited a piece of pepperoni on top of the steadily growing pile on Maddie's plate.

Maddie popped it in her mouth and winked at the little girl.

A flash of heat streaked through Aiden that he couldn't blame on the unseasonably warm September afternoon. He was seated at the other end of the table, but he'd been acutely aware of Maddie's presence during the course of the meal.

He'd told himself it was his responsibility to make sure she felt comfortable. It was becoming clear, though, that Maddie was entirely capable of holding her own.

It was also becoming clear that Aiden's first impression of her hadn't been completely accurate. Maddie was quiet, but she definitely wasn't shy. She simply listened more than she talked, drawing the people around her into conversation with just the right question or comment. And the woman he'd labeled "studious" a week ago smiled a lot, too.

Aiden found himself watching for the dimple to emerge.

He shifted so Liam's shoulder wasn't blocking his view of Maddie. He'd also described her as pretty, but that word no longer fit anymore, either.

With her tawny hair, big green eyes and perfect pink bow lips, Maddie was beautiful...although Aiden didn't think she was aware of it.

She suddenly glanced in his direction and caught him staring. A slow blush rose in her cheeks, and she quickly looked away.

Aiden wasn't sure why, but the only member of the Kane family whom Maddie seemed uncomfortable with was *him*.

Chapter Thirteen

"Maddie?"

Maddie froze at the sound of Aiden's voice behind her.

In all the after-dinner commotion, she wasn't sure Aiden would notice her absence, let alone follow her out to the car.

Maddie pasted a smile on her face before pivoting to face him. "Thank you again for inviting us to stay for pizza. I offered to help clean up, but Sunni shooed me out of the kitchen."

And right now, she needed an Aiden-free zone. Familiar surroundings where she could get her head on straight again and remember that she wasn't part of his wonderful, boisterous family. She was his…his *research assistant.*

"One of Mom's favorite sayings is 'the more the merrier.'" A breeze ticked up, ruffling Aiden's hair. "It explains why she adopted all three of us. I was wondering… can you stick around for a few more minutes?"

"I—" *Should say no. Just. Say. No. Maddie.*

"Please. I need to talk to you about something." Aiden fished around in his pocket and drew out the keys to the UTV. "In private."

He'd had to use the word *please.*

Maddie glanced at the house. If the topic of the conversation was something Aiden didn't want his family to overhear, it would explain the subtle change Maddie detected in his mood.

Now she was curious *and* concerned.

"All right."

Dodger was waiting for them, sitting patiently next to the passenger side of the side-by-side.

"Really?" Aiden scooped the dog up and set him in the middle of the seat. "We need to talk about this strange attachment you have to my UTV."

Maddie suppressed a smile. Aiden would probably deny it, but she suspected it was the man, not the machine, Dodger was getting attached to.

She waited until Aiden stowed his crutch in the back before turning the key in the ignition. "Where are we going?"

He pointed up the driveway. "That way."

An actual road Maddie could handle. She was also secretly relieved they weren't going anywhere near the shed where Aiden's brothers had stashed his pickup truck.

Maddie drove past the workshop keeping a light foot on the gas in an attempt to keep the dust down and her passengers from bouncing out of the vehicle.

Right before the wooden bridge, Aiden pointed to the left.

All Maddie saw were trees and more trees. And maybe—if she squinted—a narrow space between them.

"So…you want me to take the invisible trail into the woods now?"

His low laugh went right through Maddie and wound around her heart. Twice. "Right."

"That's what I thought." She obediently turned in that direction, even though everything inside her was clambering to return to the safety of her apartment.

The sun simmered low in the clouds, painting the sky

with delicate brushstrokes of apricot, rose and lavender that reminded Maddie of the illustrations in the Winter books.

Aiden had said he wanted to talk to her about something, but apparently he was content to wait until they reached their destination.

The terrain began to change, and a quarter mile into the woods, the fleeting patches of indigo Maddie glimpsed between the trees told her they were getting closer to the river again.

And then the trail completely disappeared.

Maddie tapped the brake and looked at Aiden for direction.

"We have to go the rest of the way on foot," he said.

Maddie searched Aiden's face, but the man who loved to joke around looked totally serious.

On foot. And Aiden didn't seem to care that only one of his was in top working condition.

"It's not far." Aiden's crooked smile told Maddie he'd read her mind. He scooped up Dodger and set the dog on the ground. "Do you see that fallen tree over there?"

Maddie saw a lot of them, but knowing Aiden, he meant the giant white pine stretched out over the river. The trunk was partially submerged in water, and the massive web of roots erupting from the ground rose almost as high as the wall she and the teenagers had built for The Pendulum.

"Is this part of the course?" Maddie kept a watchful eye on Aiden as they slowly picked their way through the brush.

"It's just a place I like to go. To think." He lifted a branch with the end of his crutch, holding it in place so Maddie could duck underneath it. "I haven't been able to get here for a while."

Maddie's favorite thinking place was the velvet wingback chair in her apartment, but this…this was nice, too.

Dodger must have agreed, because his tail began to wag as he limped toward the water.

The current had slowed here, and the reeds growing in the shallow water performed a synchronized ballet to the melody of the river.

"Take a seat." Aiden motioned toward the fallen tree. The elements had hollowed out the center, creating a natural bench where a person—Maddie's breath caught in her lungs when Aiden squeezed in beside her—*or two* could sit down.

"Cold?"

Maddie's lungs stopped working completely when Aiden stripped off his flannel shirt, leaving a T-shirt behind, and draped it around her shoulders, adding another layer of protection against the falling temperatures.

It was as if the wilderness—sunshine and fresh air and the tangy scent of pine—had been woven into the fabric. The heat from Aiden's body had warmed it, too, which should have reduced the number of goose bumps on Maddie's arms, not quadrupled them.

She was comfortable with silence—the presence of an attractive man like Aiden, not so much.

If they'd been somewhere else, the intimacy of the quiet setting would have felt like a date.

Madeline Rose. Get a grip.

"You wanted to talk to me about something?" she prompted, to remind herself that Aiden had had a specific purpose for bringing her here.

"I had an enlightening conversation with my brothers last night. It turns out Brendan's memory was a little faulty. Not the conversation he overheard, but when it took place." A quiet exhale stirred the air. "That means the timeline I gave you for our sister's birthday is wrong, too."

Maddie listened as Aiden relayed the details.

"I guess it's my fault, for taking so many trips to the ER," he joked.

Maddie saw right through his attempt at humor. The more time she spent with Aiden, the more she realized his lighthearted responses weren't meant to draw attention. He used humor to deflect it. As a shield to hide his emotions.

Finding his sister without a name or a birth date already seemed like an impossible task, and Aiden didn't want to fail.

"I emailed several adoption agencies and asked for general information about closed adoptions," Maddie told him. "I wanted to know more before I offered any details about your situation."

"Brendan and Liam are worried she doesn't want to be found, but maybe she doesn't know she has a family who's looking for her," Aiden said.

Maddie struggled to find the words that would encourage Aiden not to lose hope.

"We don't know where your sister is, but God does. The timeline is off, but we can trust *His* timing."

Aiden looked away, jaw settling into a hard line, fingers curling into fists at his side.

The posture of a child resisting the comfort of his father's arms, not leaning on him for strength.

"I thought I had the trust thing down, but..." Aiden stopped. Shook his head. "It sounds stupid. After seeing my truck, I know I should be grateful to be alive, but I can't help but wonder why—"

"He didn't spare you from the whole thing?"

Maddie's words, though softly spoken, landed like a punch to Aiden's gut.

He swung around to face her again, but the deepening shadows hid her expression from view. "How did you know that?"

"I don't think you're the only one who's asked that question when something bad happened in their life."

True. But something in Maddie's voice told Aiden she was remembering a specific situation. "What happened to you?"

He felt, rather than saw, her surprise.

"I had heart surgery after I was born," Maddie finally said. "Two of them, actually. I was in and out of the hospital while I was growing up, and my parents steered me toward activities that wouldn't put my health at risk."

"Like books."

"Like books," Maddie agreed. "I understood why Mom and Dad were so protective, but when I had to watch everyone doing the things I couldn't do, I got angry with God. I wanted to fit in but I felt...invisible. The odd girl out who really *was* odd. Everyone else in my class had perfect hearts. Why wasn't mine perfect? Didn't God care about me as much as He cared about them?"

Aiden's stomach tightened. Maddie *did* understand how he was feeling. The same dark thought had run through his mind more than once in the past few weeks.

"But you don't feel like that anymore."

"There are times I do." Maddie's quiet admission stunned him. "But I don't want to be the person who says, *If God loves me, then...* And I fill in the blank with what I want or think I should have. I want to be the one who drops the *if* and says, *God loves me, so...* His plan is always better than mine. Always for my good."

Aiden flinched. A lot of the conversations rolling around inside his head lately had started with the word *if*.

"My situation didn't change but my attitude did," Maddie went on. "I started focusing on the things I could do instead of what I couldn't. I spent so much time in the high school library, people assumed I worked there and started asking me for help." She paused and a hint of mischief tugged at the corners of her lips. "It must have been the geeky glasses. Anyway, it opened a door for a job after graduation, and when Mrs. Whitman retired, the city hired me to take her place."

Aiden wanted to tell Maddie there was nothing geeky about her glasses. He also wanted to tell her that she was wrong. The heart that Maddie claimed wasn't perfect was the same one that drew people like Tyler and Justin and Skye in.

She'd graduated a year behind him, but Aiden had no memory of Maddie in high school. Not because she'd been invisible, like she'd claimed, but because *he'd* been an idiot.

He should have hung out at the library more.

"But you're okay now, right?" Aiden tried to imagine Maddie surviving two major surgeries as an infant. "The doctors fixed your heart?"

The split second of silence that followed caused a sudden spike in Aiden's pulse.

"The surgery was a success," she finally said. "But I can't...put too much strain on it." Maddie shifted a little, opening up a space between them. "We should probably go back."

"Go back?" Aiden had had a goal in mind when he'd asked Maddie to take him to the river, but now he didn't want the evening to end. "Why?"

"The sun is going down. It's going to be dark soon."

"The moon will take over." Aiden stretched his legs out, crossed his arms behind his head and made himself more comfortable. "And if necessary, we can use your fleece jacket to find our way home."

Aiden heard an indignant little sniff. "It's not *that* bright."

"Oh. It is."

"But—"

"Listen." Short of tossing him into the UTV and making a break for the house, Aiden figured that Maddie was stuck with him for a while. The red squirrel that sounded the alarm when Dodger had dared to venture into its territory had scuttled away, and the breeze had died down so even the leaves no longer whispered in the trees. "Do you hear that?"

Maddie tipped her head. "I don't hear anything."

"Exactly." Aiden exhaled a low laugh. "In the city, you can see the moon, but the artificial light takes over. When we moved here, I couldn't believe there were this many stars. I'd sneak out at night when everyone else was asleep and lie on my back in the grass and stare up at the Milky Way for hours."

"That's the Andromeda Galaxy." Maddie's teeth sank into her lower lip, the gesture followed by a quick, sideways glance to see if she'd offended him.

Aiden chuckled. "Someone paid attention in science class."

Maddie smiled up at the shimmering puddle of light overhead. Surrounded by droplets of silver, it looked as if someone had accidentally tipped over a bucket of stars. "How Far is a Star?"

"I have no idea." Aiden's lips quirked. "Because I was the one who *didn't* pay attention in class."

"It's the title of one of my favorite books when I was little," Maddie said. "I checked it out of the library so many times that Mrs. Whitman finally told me to keep it and ordered a new copy. Pegasus got lost and had to work his way through all the constellations to find his way home."

"You remember the plot?"

"I told you I was odd."

Not odd. Pretty amazing.

"Whenever I cracked open a book, the words seemed to move around the page," Aiden told her. "It took so much effort to bring them back into focus, I stopped trying. My teachers always wrote 'not measuring up to his potential' and 'doesn't maintain focus' on my report cards, but Sunni wasn't buying it. She said if I couldn't sit down long enough to read a book, the book would have to go along with me. She recorded chapters of my textbooks, ordered books on tape, made me wear headphones when I was messing around outside."

Maddie's lips parted. "You said you didn't read."

"It wasn't a lie. Technically, what I did fell under the category of *listening*," Aiden said. "I'll never be as smart as you and Brendan, but I made it to graduation."

"Not everyone can retain information that way, so you *are* smart."

She was wrong. If Aiden had been smart, he would have noticed Maddie Montgomery way before now.

He tilted his head toward the heavens. "So where is Pegasus now? How did he find his way home?"

Maddie laughed. "I was eight years old, Aiden, and the constellations in the book were smaller than a postcard. This isn't the same."

"It's the same sky."

Maddie adjusted the glasses on her nose and scanned the heavens.

"He started over there." She mapped the shape with the tip of her finger. "The crooked row of stars…those are his front legs."

"I can see him." Aiden leaned back. "Keep reading."

Chapter Fourteen

"Maddie?" Janette Morrison leaned over the top of the circulation desk. "I keep hearing a beep."

Maddie's head jerked up, not only embarrassed the woman had caught her daydreaming but also because the "beep" Janette had heard was coming from Maddie's purse. She'd broken one of her own rules and forgotten to silence her cell phone.

It was Aiden's fault Maddie had been having a difficult time concentrating on her work this morning. And also on the road the night before, when she'd been driving home and the sky had come to life. Stretched beyond the pages of a dog-eared picture book.

The extra hour Maddie had spent pointing out the constellations to Aiden had kept her awake for at least three more after she'd returned to her apartment.

Maddie had told him the truth when she'd claimed that transferring the constellations from the simple illustrations in her memory to the black velvet canvas over their heads wasn't the same.

It was so much better.

Janette moved away, and Maddie dug the phone out of her purse. A text message from Skye popped up.

Designing T-shirts for RQ. One for you?

A simple gesture, but Maddie was so touched, tears sprang to her eyes.

She sent back a quick reply.

YES!

The landline on the circulation desk rang as Maddie was putting hers away.

"Castle Falls Library."

"May I speak with Ms. Madeline Montgomery, please?"

The feminine voice—laced with a crisp British accent—brought a smile to Maddie's lips. "This is Maddie Montgomery."

"Victoria Gerard. I'm calling in regard to the email you sent."

Maddie had sent out at least half a dozen emails to library patrons before she'd left Connie in charge on Saturday morning...and the woman's name didn't sound familiar.

"You had some questions concerning closed adoptions?" Victoria Gerard prompted.

Oh. Those emails.

Maddie's knees turned to liquid, and she sank into her chair. "I...yes. I did."

But try as she might, Maddie couldn't remember a single one. Victoria Gerard had caught her completely off guard. She'd expected a response from some of the adoption agencies she'd contacted, but had imagined it would be in the form of another email, not a phone call.

Victoria cleared her throat, and when she spoke again her tone had warmed up several degrees. "Perhaps you'd prefer to speak with one of our counselors? The Holt-McIntyre Agency has several qualified people on staff—"

"*No*," Maddie choked out. "The questions… I'm making them on behalf of a friend."

"I see," Victoria said smoothly. "Well, I'll do my best to answer them for…her."

Maddie waved goodbye to Janette Morrison as the members of the historical society filed out the door after their meeting. Fortunately, the number of people who came into the library over the noon hour dwindled, so she would be able to talk to Victoria without interruption.

But where to start?

Maddie sent up a simple yet heartfelt prayer—*help!*—and a sense of peace rolled in, taking the place of her initial panic.

"If a birth mother agreed to a closed adoption, does that mean the records are permanently sealed?" Maddie asked.

"I can't answer for other agencies, but at Holt-McIntyre, if both the child's birth parents and the adoptive parents made a contractual agreement, of course that agreement would be considered binding."

"My friend recently discovered that his sister was given up for adoption," Maddie said. "I'm reaching out to adoption agencies in your area to find out what his options are."

"There are laws governing all adoptions, but internal policies and protocol vary from agency to agency," Victoria said slowly. "At Holt-McIntyre, we are committed to protecting our clients' privacy. In the rare instance that one of the children placed in a closed adoption returns to us and makes inquiries about their birth family, our attorney meets with them to discuss the situation. If a health crisis leads to questions about the birth parents' medical history, for example."

Maddie felt her frustration rising. Victoria's responses were so smooth, so well crafted, Maddie got the impression she was reading straight from the policy manual she'd mentioned.

"But doesn't the person who's adopted have a right to know about their past?"

"A young mother and a couple came to an agreement. Made a decision in the best interests of a child unable to make a decision on their own behalf. There are many reasons why the parties both agreed to a closed adoption. You raise a valid point, Ms. Montgomery, but things aren't always that simple. I'm not sure it's a question of whether that child has a right to know…but whether they *should*."

The words hung in the silence, but Maddie wasn't quite ready to end the conversation.

"I understand the importance of privacy, but isn't there a way to let the adoptee know they have siblings who want to meet them? That wouldn't violate the agency's policy, would it?"

"I suppose it wouldn't," Victoria finally conceded. "But our director would still want to review the case before she agreed."

Maddie wanted to question why the agency thought it was necessary to maintain such tight control, but she wasn't about to say anything that would upset the woman on the other end of the line.

"The baby was a girl," Maddie said. "We're not sure of her exact birth date, but she would be in her early to midtwenties now. Her biological mother's name was Carla Kane."

In the brief silence that followed, Maddie assumed that Victoria was jotting the information down. But when it stretched out for another ten seconds, she wondered if they'd been cut off.

"Hello? Ms. Gerard—"

"I'll pass this information on to our director," Victoria cut Maddie off. "Have a good day, Ms. Montgomery."

"Thank—" *You.*

Victoria had already ended the call.

Maddie's heart sank as she put the phone down.

She'd tried to be assertive, not argumentative, but it was obvious she'd failed.

Because the woman Maddie had been so careful to avoid upsetting had sounded…upset.

"Here you go, Aiden. Three scoops of rocky road." Anna handed Aiden a cone stacked high with his favorite ice cream.

"Even though it's Monday, not Triple Scoop Tuesday," Liam reminded him.

"Don't be bitter, bro." A stopover at The Happy Cow had become a weekly tradition whenever it was Anna's turn to pick Aiden up from physical therapy. Today, the therapist had announced that his appointments were being reduced to once a week and provided a list of follow-up exercises Aiden could continue at home. "We're celebrating. Don't you see the sprinkles on top?"

Liam rolled his eyes. "You spoil him."

"Of course she does. Thanks, Anna." He winked at her. "You're my favorite almost-sister-in-law."

Anna chuckled. "I should thank you for not minding hanging out here for a little while. Liam's been so busy lately we haven't had a chance to meet with Pastor Seth for our premarital counseling. When he had an opening in his schedule this afternoon, we didn't want to turn it down."

Aiden knew it wasn't Anna's intention to make him feel guilty, but he still felt the pinch. The extra work River Quest had created was part of the reason his brother had been so busy.

There were still moments Aiden wished he would have scrapped the whole thing and given the teams who'd registered a refund.

But where would that have left Tyler and Justin? And Skye, for that matter.

"I doubt my brother minds hanging out at an ice-cream shop." Liam chuckled. "Just don't eat all the proceeds while we're gone, okay?"

Aiden's gaze strayed to the brick building on the corner of the opposite side of the street. "It's a nice day," he said casually. "I'll probably take a walk or something."

"Or something?" Liam's eyebrow shot up. "Like check out a book, maybe?"

Anna grinned.

Rats. Aiden had returned to the house the night before only to find Sunni sitting in the living room, waiting up for him like he was Tyler and Justin's age and still on a curfew.

She hadn't asked many questions, though, which was a little suspicious. Now he understood why. His mom didn't need Aiden to fill in the details because she'd already formed her own conclusion. A conclusion Sunni had no doubt shared with the rest of his nosy family.

"Checking out a book usually involves a library card," Aiden said. "Which I don't have. And even if I did, the library closes in a few minutes."

Liam tilted his head. "Anna, isn't it strange that a person who doesn't have a library card knows what the hours of said library are?"

"Very strange," she agreed, her eyes sparkling.

Aiden shooed them toward the door with his crutch. "Go. Get counseling. I'll see you in an hour."

He waited until Anna's van peeled away from the curb and rumbled out of sight before venturing outside.

The fall festival was a little over a week away, but the businesses on Riverside were already starting to prepare for the event. The owner of CJ's Variety had parked an antique wagon filled with pumpkins in front of a plate-glass window overlooking the street, and the chamber of commerce had hung pots of yellow and bronze mums from the lampposts—attractive additions designed to draw visitors to the town and encourage the locals to gather together and enjoy autumn's breathtaking display of natural fireworks before the long winter set in.

Aiden paused to study a poster that listed the activities in the window of the coffee shop next door. The lineup looked the same as it did every year. A craft fair. The chili cook-off and live music in the park. A chain of food booths that featured everything from apple fritters on a stick to the traditional pasty, a handheld meat pie that Cornish miners had introduced to the area in the 1800s.

Near the bottom of the poster, Aiden saw the Castle Falls Outfitters' logo superimposed over a picture of the river.

Lily's doing, of course, but Aiden hadn't known they'd put money into advertising River Quest.

Another layer of guilt added to the weight he had already been carrying.

Sure, they'd reached the maximum number of teams for the competition, but River Quest would be a true success only if spectators came to watch it, too. If those spectators browsed for souvenirs in the Trading Post and filled next season's calendar with guided trips down the river.

If Brendan and Liam finally began to see him as a valued partner instead of their kid brother.

Aiden shook that thought away as he turned from the window, but it wasn't as easy to ignore the ones that crowded in to take its place.

What if he'd made another mistake? What if River Quest ended up costing more money than it brought in?

Aiden crossed the street, retraced a path that was already becoming as familiar as the one he'd taken through the woods with Maddie the night before.

In the past, staring up at the stars while the river played music in the background smoothed the ragged edges of

Aiden's soul. But last night, it was the woman sitting next to him who had instilled a sense of peace.

And panic.

Aiden hadn't known those two emotions could coexist. But then again, that was before he'd met Maddie.

He liked spending time with her, but Aiden wasn't sure she felt the same way about him.

According to the clock in the bank tower, the library should be closed. But lights glowed in the window and—Aiden turned the handle on the door—the building was still unlocked.

Maddie wasn't behind the circulation desk, and the chairs in the reading nook were empty.

Aiden was about to call Maddie's name, quietly of course, when he heard a low giggle on the other side of the bookshelves that formed a colorful hedge around the children's area.

He decided to investigate, the ladybug rug absorbing the tread of his footsteps as he followed the sound to its source.

A young woman in a lavender dress sat on a plastic chair, as still as a statue, while a girl about five or six years old carefully arranged a crown of plastic daisies in her hair.

It took a moment for Aiden to realize the woman was Maddie.

Tawny hair flowed over her shoulders, all the way down to the center of her back.

He forgot how to breathe. All Aiden could do was open and close his mouth a few times, as helpless as a landed trout.

"We're playing princess!" The little girl spotted Aiden before he could back out of sight and regroup.

Maddie twisted around in the chair, and a tide of red flooded her cheeks when their eyes met.

"Aiden. W-what are you doing here?"

He dragged in a breath and forced it out again. "I was

waiting for Anna and Liam and thought I'd stop by and—" *And what, Aiden? Make it sound legit.* "Say hi?"

It probably would have sounded more legitimate if Aiden hadn't phrased it in the form of a question.

"Hi!" The little girl saved him from the awkward moment with a gap-toothed grin. "My name's Isabella but Gramma and Daddy call me *Bea* sometimes. What's your name?"

Thanks to Anna's twins, Aiden had gotten pretty good at following the conversational twists and turns of the under-ten set. "Aiden."

"That's a nice name," she pronounced before pointing to the circle of plastic daisies listing over Maddie's forehead. "I made a crown for Miss Maddie. Isn't it pretty?"

"Very pretty," Aiden agreed, unable to pull his gaze away from the woman sitting in the chair.

Maddie shifted, clearly uncomfortable as the center of attention. Aiden, on the other hand, liked seeing this whimsical side of her. She'd be a great mom someday.

He bent down until he and the little girl were eye to eye. "There's only one thing missing," he whispered.

"What?" she whispered back.

"Her wings."

Two bright blue eyes rounded on him. "Wings?"

"This princess is really a pixie in disguise. And pixies," he said solemnly, "always have wings. She must have misplaced hers."

"I'll look in the dress-up box!" Maddie's pint-size fairy godmother had taken only two dancing steps toward an antique steamer trunk in the corner when the door opened again.

"Isabella?"

"We're back here, Gramma!" The girl went up on her tiptoes and waved her arms in the air.

A trim blonde woman close to Sunni's age appeared a

moment later. “I’m so sorry, Maddie,” she said without preamble. “There was a line a mile long at the grocery store, and then I realized I’d left my checkbook in the car…”

“That’s all right.” Maddie smiled. “It gave me and Isabella time to find a book about ponies.”

“My mom had a pony when she was my age, didn’t she, Gramma?” Isabella locked her arms around her grandmother’s knee. “When Daddy gets home from work, I’m going to show him the book and ask if I can have one, too!”

The wrinkles fanning out from the woman’s eyes seemed to deepen. “Your daddy won’t be home until after you’re asleep.” She gently clasped Isabella’s shoulders and turned her toward Maddie. “Now, what do you say to Miss Maddie?”

Another gap-toothed grin. “Thank you!”

Maddie returned the smile and handed Isabella a book with a bright-eyed pony on the cover. “I’ll see you next week.”

“The bed-and-breakfast is full between now and the fall festival, so it may be a little longer than that. Not that I’m complaining,” the girl’s grandmother added quickly. “Without guests, the beds would be empty and we’d have to eat all the pancakes ourselves. Wouldn’t we, Bea?”

“That’s okay!” Isabella skipped away. “I love pancakes!”

The woman mouthed the words “thank you” to Maddie and followed her toward the door.

After they’d gone, Aiden cocked a brow. “Babysitting is part of your job description, too?”

“Not very often, but sometimes a mom—or a grandma, in Karen Bristow’s case—asks permission to run a quick errand while their child looks for a book.”

“Bristow?” Aiden repeated. “As in Deputy Bristow?”

Maddie nodded. “Karen is his mother. She’s the one

who brings Isabella to the library, though, so I've never met Carter or his wife."

Aiden didn't know anything about Carter Bristow's background, but he couldn't quite see it. The granite-jawed officer didn't exactly give off warm, fuzzy vibes that screamed "family man."

Aiden picked up a jaunty felt hat decorated with a peacock feather that had fallen on the floor. "Is this yours? Or does it go in the dress-up trunk… Maddie?" He watched as she sent a waterfall of beaded necklaces cascading off the edge of the puzzle table onto the floor. "Are you looking for something?"

"Trying," Maddie muttered. "That's the problem." She swept up a handful of hair that had fallen across her cheek and tucked it behind one ear. Without the barrette holding it place, though, the attempt proved as futile as trying to change the course of the river.

"What does that…" Aiden suddenly realized that something other than Maddie's bun was missing. "Your glasses."

"Isabella." The flash of that intriguing dimple tempered Maddie's sigh. "She insisted that princesses can't be nearsighted."

Aiden grinned. "In that case, you'd better let me take over the search."

After a brief time, he found them underneath a pink feather boa on the lower shelf of a bookcase.

"Here you go."

Maddie reached for them, but Aiden shook his head. "I'm surprised you can read anything through these smudges." He scrubbed at the lens with the tail of his shirt. "Here. Good as new."

Maddie looked up at the same time Aiden looked down, leaving less than an inch of space between them. He had a close-up view of her gold-tipped lashes. The exact place where the green in her eyes deepened to emerald.

The air in the room changed, and Aiden's pulse picked up speed, the way it did whenever he was about to embark on a new adventure. Only Aiden had the strangest feeling this adventure wasn't taking him farther from home. It was bringing him *closer.*

"Maddie?" Aiden breathed her name, and the tiny gap between them began to disappear as he bent his head…

"Miss M? Are you here?"

Skye.

Aiden stifled a groan as Maddie plucked the glasses out of his hand and fled.

Chapter Fifteen

"Unless you have any questions, I think that's all for tonight."

Maddie shut down her laptop, and the last image on the PowerPoint disappeared.

After spending countless hours over the past two weeks trying to get the teenagers in her charge to pay attention, *she* was the one who'd had trouble concentrating during their Monday study session.

Maddie had never felt so relieved—or so disappointed—in her life when she'd heard Skye's voice.

Aiden had left a few minutes after the girl had arrived, allowing Maddie to take her first full breath since he'd shown up unannounced at the library.

The man had a penchant for catching her off guard.

Being content with her life had been easy until Aiden Kane had limped through the front door of the library that day and turned it upside down. First with his request for help and take-no-prisoners smile…and last night, when Maddie had caught a rare glimpse of the man behind that smile. Protective. Fiercely devoted to his family, to the point where he wasn't afraid to step out and take risks.

And then this afternoon, when he'd almost kissed her.

The knot in Maddie's stomach tightened.

Not because Aiden had almost kissed her—because Maddie would have kissed him right back.

But when a person had to outweigh the cost against the risk—and the outcome of that risk was uncertain—wasn't it better to leave things the way they were?

Aiden apparently didn't think so, because he was intent on finding their younger sister.

Maddie closed her eyes. She hadn't had an opportunity to tell Aiden about her conversation with Victoria Gerard earlier that day, either. Not that there was much to tell. The woman hadn't been exactly encouraging about the search.

"Miss M?"

Maddie started at the sound of Tyler's voice. She thought he'd left with Justin and Skye after their meeting.

As preoccupied as Maddie had been throughout the evening, she hadn't missed the fact that Tyler had been looking at his cell phone more than the handouts Maddie had passed out.

"Did you have a question about the material we covered tonight, Tyler?"

"No…" The floor creaked underneath his weight as he rocked from foot to foot. "I have an idea for a topic."

"That's wonderful!" Outwardly, Maddie smiled. Inwardly, she sent up a silent, heartfelt *Thank you, Lord.* During her weekly update with the principal, he'd expressed reservations about the amount of time the boys and Skye were devoting to River Quest instead of their homework.

Maddie, who'd tried her best to convince him that spending time at Castle Falls Outfitters *was* homework, realized the proof she needed would be in the form of the topics for their senior presentations.

Skye and Justin had both handed in the assignment, but Tyler had slumped lower in the chair and avoided Maddie's eyes.

He *still* wouldn't look her in the eye, but Maddie sensed a subtle change in the boy's attitude. She'd grown accustomed to brusque, but now Tyler appeared almost bashful.

"So...are you going to tell me what it is?" she prompted when the boy remained silent.

"My dad."

"Your dad?" Maddie repeated cautiously. In all the previous years she'd worked with students from the high school, Maddie couldn't remember anyone choosing a person as the focus for the senior project.

"He—" Tyler's Adam's apple convulsed. "He worked for a logging company, and a few years ago, one of the trees they were cutting down split in half when it fell. Dad didn't have a chance to get out of the way. It... He ended up losing both legs from the knees down."

Maddie struggled to conceal her shock. "I'm so sorry, Tyler. I had no idea."

"Why would you?" The boy shrugged. "Dad doesn't get out much. He doesn't like anyone staring or fussing over him. Mom works as a sales rep and travels a lot, so I kind of keep an eye on things at home."

Even though Tyler spoke the words matter-of-factly, it wasn't difficult to read between the lines. Suddenly Maddie understood why Tyler was constantly looking at his phone. He wasn't on social media or playing games. He was checking in with his dad.

She also understood the reason his grades had been slipping. Tyler bore the weight of so much responsibility at home, was it any wonder he had trouble keeping up with school?

"And I convinced you to participate in River Quest, so now you're away from home even more."

"Uh-huh." Tyler's quick nod did nothing to assuage Maddie's guilt. "I wasn't going to tell Dad about it. Before he got hurt, he lived for the weekends when he could be outside. Go fishing and hunting. I was afraid if I told him about River Quest, he'd feel bad because he couldn't do those things anymore. But Dad cornered me last night because he was afraid I was getting into trouble. Like I have time, right?" Tyler's eyes rolled toward the ceiling in a gesture that, to Maddie, appeared more affectionate than frustrated. "I thought Dad would make me quit, but when I told him what I've been doing, all he said was that he wished he could be in the canoe with me. It got me thinking...why couldn't he? Maybe he can't compete in River Quest, but did you know there are all kinds of competitions designed for people in wheelchairs?"

Maddie's eyes burned. "I've heard of those."

"So that's what my presentation is going to be about." Tyler hesitated. "I thought maybe I could talk to Aiden about modifying the course next year. You know, so people like my dad could enter."

"I think—" Maddie swallowed around the lump in her throat "—that's a great idea. And I'm sure Aiden will think so, too."

"Ten minutes and fifteen seconds." Aiden held up the stopwatch as Tyler and Justin glided toward the riverbank. In his canoe.

"Is that good?" Justin asked.

"Added to the rest of your time, I'd say you're right on track."

Tyler came off his seat in the stern and pumped one fist in the air. "Did you get video, Skye?"

"I got it." The girl held up the camera as proof. "And if you keep rocking the canoe like that, I'll have another addition to the blooper reel."

Aiden twisted toward her. "Blooper reel?"

"Don't worry." Skye grinned. "You're not on it. Much."

He glanced at Maddie for confirmation the girl was teasing, but she was already walking down to the shoreline.

The fact Skye hadn't added him to the blooper reel didn't mean he hadn't made one at the library the day before.

Maddie had kept her promise to the teenagers and brought them over for another training session on Friday after school, but the woman who'd sat shoulder to shoulder with Aiden, watching God's spectacular nighttime show, was all business. Polite and yet as distant as the stars she'd named.

Aiden had crossed a line in the library when he'd almost kissed Maddie, but the only thing he regretted was that it hadn't actually happened.

The electricity that charged the air whenever they were together was more than simple chemistry. Aiden had been attracted to women in the past, but when it came to Maddie, what he felt was more than the spark of physical attraction. It was something deeper, kindling the kind of fire that could last a lifetime, if tended properly.

But maybe that was the problem. With all the junk in his past, maybe she didn't see him as a forever kind of guy.

"What do you think?" Tyler loomed in front of Aiden, soaked to the skin but grinning. "Do we have a chance?"

Aiden's gaze slid to Maddie for what had to be the hundredth time over the past few hours. "Rich, my foster dad, told me that the only person guaranteed to fail is the one who gives up."

Advice he should apply to his own life.

Sunni had planned a cookout for supper, and there were five extra chairs around the fire pit. If his mom was doing her matchmaker thing, Aiden didn't mind. With Maddie, he needed all the help he could get.

Dodger, who considered himself an honorary member of the Flamethrowers, suddenly stopped dead in his tracks.

Tyler followed suit, pulling up so fast that Aiden almost crashed into him.

"Hey—"

"What's he doing here?"

Aiden followed an invisible line between Tyler's frown and a squad car parked in front of the house. Sunni stood next to the vehicle, deep in conversation with a tall, dark-haired county deputy. Even at a distance, Aiden recognized Carter Bristow.

"The sheriff's department likes to stay ahead of things that might impact the community during the fall festival," Aiden said. "This is the first time we've hosted one of the events, so he's probably checking in with Sunni about River Quest."

Tyler's scowl faded, but so did the spring in his step as Bristow's attention shifted toward them. His expression didn't change, but Aiden suspected the deputy had the ability to gather all the intel he needed from one single, assessing glance.

Sunni beckoned them closer with a wave and a smile, gathering the teenagers into a loose half circle that no one looked particularly eager to join. "Aiden, this is Deputy Bristow."

"We've met." Aiden reached out and shook Carter's hand. "Deputy."

Carter inclined his head. "Ribs still giving you trouble, huh?"

"Sometimes." And here Aiden thought he'd been hiding it so well. Did the guy have a background in medicine, too?

"Aiden has been coaching one of the teams before River Quest." When all three team members shuffled their feet and looked down at the ground, Sunni turned to Maddie. "And this is Maddie Montgomery."

Recognition flickered briefly in the deputy's eyes. "The librarian."

"It's nice to meet you." Maddie smiled. "I've enjoyed getting to know Isabella during story time. I might have to adjust the budget so I can order more books about horses."

Isabella—the little girl who'd set a crown of daisies in Maddie's hair.

Aiden would have never guessed the bubbly, pony-loving princess and the stern, no-nonsense cop were related. Isabella and Carter Bristow shared the same last name, but there was no physical resemblance between the father and daughter that Aiden could see. The deputy had dark hair and eyes, as striking as sunlight against shadow compared with the little girl's golden-blond curls and sky blue eyes.

When Carter acknowledged Maddie's teasing comment with a curt nod, it was obvious he and his daughter had different temperaments, too.

The deputy turned back to Aiden. "Could I have a few minutes of your time?"

"Sure." Aiden wasn't nearly as skilled at reading people as a police officer, but if Carter needed details about Castle Falls Outfitters' involvement in the fall festival, he could have gotten the information from Sunni.

"Everyone else can go up to the house and wash up," Sunni said cheerfully. "Liam has the grill going, so all you have to do is put your order in."

The teenagers didn't have to be told twice. Maddie started after them, and it was only by clamping his back teeth together that Aiden was able to override the overwhelming—and completely ridiculous—impulse to beg the woman who'd spent the majority of the afternoon keeping her distance to stay with him.

He could only hope that Bristow's law enforcement training had focused on reading people's body language, not their minds.

To Aiden's relief, Carter wasn't looking at him at all. He was staring down at Dodger.

"He looks good." The deputy sounded surprised. "If it wasn't for the snarl, I wouldn't have recognized him."

"It's a *smile...*" Aiden stopped. "You two know each other?"

"I was the one who brought him to the vet. I didn't realize he'd ended up with you, though."

"Dodger is only here while he recuperates, and then Sunni plans to find him a good home."

"Dodger, huh?" Carter's eyebrows lifted.

"I have to call him something when he takes off with my pillow," Aiden grumbled. "Now, what is it you wanted to talk to me about?"

Carter's gaze shifted to the group of people gathered in the backyard. "Can we go somewhere private?"

"Sure. The concrete bunker under the house or the Trading Post?" Aiden wasn't sure why he enjoyed needling him, except that no-nonsense guys like Carter and Brendan needed a little loosening up once in a while.

"The Trading Post works for now," Carter said drily.

"Good, because I was kidding about the bunker." There *was* a room underneath the house, but it was Sunni's root cellar, its shelves lined with the homemade jams and salsa she canned every fall.

Bristow followed him inside the building and waited until Aiden closed the door before he spoke. "A few days ago, a hunter called dispatch and reported that he'd witnessed two vehicles racing on Razorback Road."

"Racing?" On Razor Road? Aiden had a hard time believing anyone would be that stupid.

"It's the second complaint we've had this week. Someone left an anonymous message on the tip line last night, claiming they'd been passed by two vehicles moving so fast they didn't have a chance to get license plate numbers."

"I'll talk to my brothers, but I haven't witnessed anything like that out here," Aiden told him.

"Are you sure about that?"

Aiden suddenly realized what Carter was getting at. "You think one of the drivers ran me off the road that night?"

"It would explain why he didn't stop to help you."

It sure would. And if the deputy was right, it would prove once and for all that he'd been telling the truth.

"So what happens next?" Aiden was ready to set up his own stakeout if necessary.

"I've got some names I'm checking into. Kids who've been in trouble before, looking for an adrenaline rush," Carter said. "Sometimes, all it takes is finding the one who will turn on his buddies in order to save his own skin."

"I hope you do...and I hope whoever's responsible thinks about what he did while he's sitting in jail." Aiden couldn't keep the bitterness from creeping into his voice. "I could have died that night."

A shadow passed through Carter's eyes. "I'm a firm believer that a person should be held responsible for their actions."

Aiden exhaled a slow breath.

"Yeah. Me, too."

Chapter Sixteen

On Saturday afternoon, Maddie sat on the floor cross-legged, sorting through a box of paperbacks people had donated for the book sale the weekend of the fall festival.

Maddie had come up with the idea the year she'd taken over as head librarian, and the sale proved so popular, the chamber of commerce had started to include it on the poster with the other events. Whatever the reason—whether people were anticipating a long winter or because the library's booth was wedged between two popular food stands—the books sold as fast as the café's apple cider doughnuts.

Maddie set a cozy mystery aside. As the librarian, she had the added perk of previewing the books before they went on the cart, and the mysteries, like chocolate, happened to be her weakness. The heroines weren't always beautiful, but they were smart and resourceful and brave.

At the moment, though, Maddie had to settle for two out of three.

In her first act of cowardice, she'd apologized to Sunni for not being able to stay for the cookout the night before and then slipped away while Aiden was talking to Carter Bristow. The second was when Skye had texted her earlier that morning, letting her know Aiden had invited the boys over to practice again, and Maddie had told the girl she had to put in a few extra hours at work.

Maddie *had* been neglecting the donation box over the past few weeks, but the task wasn't so overwhelming she'd had to tackle it over the weekend. No, what Maddie needed was a little distance from Aiden.

What she hadn't realized was that the very place she'd always found peace would remind her of him, too.

Ordinarily, she sorted through the donations in the children's area because it had a lot of space and a comfortable rug. Today she'd spent the afternoon trying to forget how embarrassed she'd been stumbling about without her glasses.

Trying to forget the way Aiden had looked at her. The brush of his fingers against her cheek.

The door of the library opened, and Maddie's heart plummeted all the way down to the red ballet slippers on her feet.

She peeked around the bookshelf just in time to see Anna and Lily breeze in.

"Hey, girl!" Lily spotted her immediately. "Oops." She winced and looked around. "Is there anyone else here? Should I be whispering?"

"No, the summer hours ended last week, so the library closed at two o'clock." Maddie rose to her feet. "What brings you into town this afternoon?"

Cars had lined Riverside Avenue since Maddie had unlocked the door of the library that morning. With only a week until the official start of the Fall Festival, it seemed like everyone in Castle Falls had gotten swept up in preparations for the upcoming celebration.

"You," Anna said promptly.

"Me?"

"A little bird mentioned you were getting ready for the annual book sale. We thought maybe you could use a hand." Anna and Lily exchanged a mischievous smile. "Or four, as the case may be."

Maddie wondered if the "little bird" had lavender stripes in her feathers. "I couldn't ask—"

"You didn't," Anna interrupted cheerfully. "Our guys are busy finishing the course for River Quest, and Sunni took the twins over to Rebecca's house for their final dress fitting—"

"So we decided to spend the afternoon here," Lily cut in.

Maddie was confused. "Sorting through books at the library?"

"Quality girl time with friends," Lily corrected.

It took Maddie a second to realize that included her.

Anna patted the bulging tote bag looped over her shoulder. "We even brought the necessary supplies."

"Chocolate," Lily whispered, even though she didn't have to.

"So…tell us what to do." Anna's tote hit the floor with a muffled thump.

Maddie pointed to the donation boxes that lined the aisle. "Can you separate fact from fiction?"

Anna laughed. "Most of the time."

"So can I!" Lily said. "So let's break out the lemonade and start sorting." She looped her arm through Maddie's. "If we work fast, we can sneak into The Happy Cow and raid the freezer. I know people."

Anna winked at them. "And I just happen to have a key."

Maddie gave in. Anna and Lily got right down to work—except it didn't feel like work. Maddie couldn't remember the last time she'd sat in a circle on the floor with women her age and laughed until her stomach hurt. Maybe because this was the first time.

Lily held up a children's picture book. "I should buy this one for Brendan." She flashed an impish grin. "The basset on the cover looks just like our dog, Missy."

Anna's giggle told Maddie she was privy to an inside joke, but Lily quickly shared the details. "Sunni has a knack for matching up pets and people. That's how Brendan ended up with Missy."

Anna's eyes twinkled. "And Lily."

"And me," Lily agreed with a contented sigh. "Sunni denies it of course, but Brendan claims she was the mastermind behind that matchmaking scheme, too. She believes in the healing power of love."

"The pets *could* be a cover," Anna whispered.

"Brendan would call them accomplices." Lily laughed. "The man didn't want to deal with anything that wasn't on his calendar, so he didn't know what to do with me or Missy. Brendan was definitely a Mr. Darcy. Tall, dark and brooding."

Maddie, who'd never heard the story behind Brendan and Lily's romance, listened in fascination as Lily recounted the summer Sunni had hired her to renovate her home while she was on vacation.

"I thought you'd worked at a marketing firm," Maddie said.

"I did. But I took over my friend Shelby's renovation business when she got Lyme disease." Lily's expression softened. "I didn't know the first thing about renovation, but she needed help until her symptoms were under control."

"Shelby?"

"My best friend." Lily set a book with a damaged cover to one side. "We grew up in the same neighborhood. I was an only child, so Shelby was more like a sister. There were no secrets between us. We told each other everything."

Maddie's hands closed around the book in her lap as an idea began to form.

Maybe instead of searching for the adoption agency where Carla Kane had placed Aiden's sister, she should focus her efforts on finding the one person Carla might have confided in about her pregnancy.

A best friend…

Lily's chuckle drew Maddie back into the conversation. Maddie had to suppress the temptation to share her epiphany with the other women because she wasn't sure how much Aiden had told them about the search for their missing sister.

"Missy eventually won Brendan over and I have to admit—" a dreamy look stole into Lily's violet eyes "—there's something very appealing about a man who has a soft spot for dogs."

"Or a litter of kittens." The same expression came over Anna's face. "And a precocious set of twins."

"That was no accident, either." Lily rocked back on her heels. "Sunni knew those kittens would be twin bait, just like she knew Aiden needed Dodger to keep him company so he wouldn't go crazy from the forced inactivity."

"I don't know…" Anna mused. "Aiden seems to have plenty of company these days."

Now Anna and Lily were smiling at her.

Oh, *no.*

"We're just…working together for a common goal," Maddie protested. "Besides that, Aiden doesn't seem like the kind of guy who wants to settle down."

"I thought the same thing until I got to know him," Anna said. "Liam was afraid of falling in love because he didn't want to turn out like their father. Aiden is just the opposite. He's going to prove he can get it right. And you can tell he has the heart of a family man when he interacts with the twins."

Maddie could see it every time he interacted with the teenagers, too.

But the thought of Aiden falling in love and looking up at the stars with someone else made her heart ache.

She drew in a shaky breath and pushed out a smile. "I think we're done here. What were you saying about ice cream?"

On Tuesday afternoon, Aiden was setting flags out to mark the expanded parking area when Dodger, who'd been watching him work from a comfortable spot in the shade, let out a growl.

Aiden glanced over his shoulder to find out whom the dog was greeting, and saw Skye and Tyler striding across the lawn.

"Hey." He plucked his bandanna from the back pocket of his jeans and swiped at the beads of moisture on his forehead. "Aren't you two supposed to be in school?"

"We got permission to leave during study hall." Skye speared her hands deeper into the pockets of her coat, similar in style to the one Maddie had worn the week before.

Aiden stifled a smile. He wondered if Maddie even realized her influence had extended to the girl's fashion choices.

"You can call the office if you don't believe us." Tyler's chin jutted forward, the angle of his jaw as sharp as his tone.

Aiden frowned. He hadn't seen Tyler go on the defensive like this since the first week they'd met. And he'd spent enough time with the boy lately to recognize there was more behind the attitude than a blatant disregard for authority.

"I believe you," Aiden said evenly. "What's going on?"

"Ask Justin," Tyler spit out. "He's the one who pulled out of River Quest."

"What?" Dodger's low whine told Aiden he'd spoken more loudly than he'd intended.

"He bailed on us Saturday afternoon and never showed up at the library for our meeting last night, either," Skye chimed in.

Tyler nodded. "We were supposed to go over our strategy for the course one more time. I texted him, and he shot back a message telling us to go ahead without him because he wasn't going to do it anymore."

"And he didn't say why?"

"I tried calling him but I couldn't get through. He'd turned off his phone." Tyler didn't look angry. He looked like he'd been betrayed by his best friend.

"He skipped school today, too," Skye huffed. "I have a friend who works in the office, and she said that Justin was marked unexcused."

Aiden tried to hide his mounting concern. Justin had been as pumped about the competition as Tyler, and cutting class seemed out of character for the boy who'd recently asked for Maddie's help filling out college scholarship applications.

"Does Maddie know about this?"

"I texted her during lunch, but when Ty and I stopped at the library, she wasn't there," Skye said. "The lady behind the desk told us that Maddie had taken the rest of the afternoon off. We thought she'd be here."

The sudden burn in Aiden's cheeks had nothing to do with the heat of the sun. "I haven't talked to Maddie since Friday night."

Not for lack of trying, though. Maddie had skipped out on the cookout and been a no-show on Saturday. On Sunday morning, she'd volunteered in the church nursery.

Ever since that moment in the library when he'd almost kissed her, it seemed as though Maddie had been keeping her distance. Aiden could claim he'd lost his head… except that for the first time in a long time, it felt like he finally had it on straight.

"Maybe Maddie drove to Justin's house." Skye brightened. "To get him to change his mind."

"I hope so." Tyler kicked at a loose clump of grass. "I

don't want to have to tell my dad that I'm not going to be in the competition."

"Hey, let's not jump the gun." Aiden pressed a steadying hand against the boy's shoulder. "I'll track Maddie down and see if I can find out what's going on while you two head back to class."

Skye and Tyler exchanged a look, but Aiden didn't give them a chance to give him any pushback. "Where does Justin live?"

"About three miles from Razor Road," Skye said. "It's the white house set back from the road."

"I've seen it." Aiden wouldn't have guessed someone actually lived there, though. The yard was a patchwork of bare spots and weeds, and the poor condition of the house, with its crumbling foundation and sagging porch, only added to the aura of neglect. "And don't worry. With River Quest next weekend, Justin might simply have a case of cold feet."

Skye and Tyler still looked worried, but they trudged back to the car.

Aiden punched in Maddie's number as soon as the teenagers drove away, but it went straight to voice mail.

He went back to the house, grabbed the keys to Sunni's Subaru and thanked God the therapist had cleared him to drive after their last session.

Maddie would say this was proof of God's perfect timing.

Aiden smiled. He was more convinced than ever that Maddie was part of that timing, too.

He just needed an opportunity to convince her.

Maddie knocked on the door again.

She thought she'd seen the curtains move when she'd pulled up to Justin's house, but no one had answered the door.

She'd read Skye's text message three times before the meaning had sunk in.

Justin had dropped out of the competition.

Maddie could only imagine how upset his other teammates must be. The video footage Skye took during River Quest would make up the bulk of her senior presentation. And Tyler…he'd become a different kid once he'd come up with something that could help his dad.

She was also worried about Justin. He'd skipped their Monday night meeting, but scheduling conflicts weren't that unusual. Now she was afraid the reason was connected to his decision to drop out of River Quest.

Lord, everything has been going so well. The kids have been doing great...this can't fall apart now.

Maddie stepped backward and felt the boards sink underneath her feet. Her heart sank right along with it. Justin had never talked about his family, but the paint sloughing off the window frames and the crumbling foundation hinted there was no money for general maintenance, let alone improvements to the property.

Following an impulse she couldn't explain, Maddie walked around the back of the house to see if there was another entrance. Before she'd reached the door, a soft but distinct *thump* came from inside a weathered shed near the edge of the yard.

Maddie headed in that direction. The door was open a crack, and she peeked inside. Sunlight streamed through the rafters, illuminating the dust motes suspended in the air. Her gaze traveled over an ancient lawn mower and bicycle parts and landed on… Justin.

He stood in the shadows, hands rolled into fists at his side, poised for flight. Maddie had no doubt he would already be gone if she wasn't blocking the only escape avenue.

"Maddie," he croaked. "What are you doing here?"

"I wanted to talk to you. Skye and Tyler said you'd changed your mind about River Quest," Maddie said cautiously.

"Yeah?" Justin shoved his hands in his pockets. "So what?"

Maddie inwardly flinched. She'd never heard Justin use that tone of voice. "I know how excited you were about it… Did something happen?"

"I changed my mind, that's what happened."

"You're Tyler's teammate. If you pull out of the competition, he will probably have to forfeit, too," Maddie said slowly.

Justin's gaze dropped to the floor. "Skye can take my place."

"Skye won't be able to compete in the competition and record it, too." Maddie dodged a dusty skein of cobwebs hanging over the door and took a tentative step forward.

"I don't care. Not my problem."

The anguish in Justin's eyes told a different story.

"What about your senior presentation?" Knowing that Justin had asked her about college applications the last time they'd met, Maddie tried a different tact. "If you want to get into an engineering program, designing a course tailored for people with physical disabilities could result in a scholarship."

"I'm not going to college," Justin said flatly.

"Oh, Justin." Maddie's heart ached. She was more convinced than ever he hadn't changed his mind about River Quest or college on a whim. Something was very wrong. "If you can't tell me what's going on, then talk to Aiden—"

"No."

The vehemence in the word propelled Maddie back a step. "Aiden cares about you. He would want to help."

"No. He wouldn't. Not if he knew…" Justin stopped, scraped his hands down his face. "I… I can't."

Maddie wasn't sure where all this was coming from, but she did know one thing.

Can't was very different from *won't*.

Chapter Seventeen

Aiden stood frozen outside the door of the shed. He'd heard Maddie's voice, but Justin's he almost didn't recognize.

Anger never travels alone, Rich had told him. And what Aiden heard underneath the anger was guilt.

But why?

God, I'm not as smart as Brendan or as sensitive as Liam, so I could use some help here.

When Aiden opened his eyes, he saw the truck parked underneath an old lean-to in the patchy grass. At first glance, the vehicle looked as old as the house. Rust covered the body, creeping over the doors and fanning out on the hood like moss on a tree stump. But someone had jacked up the frame with oversize tires, shined up the chrome. An attempt to stand out from the crowd.

Aiden pulled in a breath so sharp he almost cracked another rib.

As a teenager, he'd painted flames on the side of his canoe in an attempt to stand out, too. To prove that Aiden Kane wasn't weak or afraid. That he was *someone*, and not a mistake.

Blindly, he pushed open the door of the shed and walked inside.

"Aiden."

Maddie's surprise changed to relief, but it was the flash of fear on Justin's face that confirmed Aiden's suspicions.

Bile rose up in his throat.

This kid, the one he'd coached and teased and cheered on, had been responsible for the accident that had almost killed him.

"I have to go somewhere." Justin tried a quarterback sneak around Maddie, but Aiden had pulled that maneuver a few times on his brothers and knew how to block it.

"What's the hurry? Late for another race?"

"Race?" The color drained from Justin's face. "I—I don't know what you're talking a-about."

"I think you do. You got worried when Deputy Bristow came over Friday night and figured it was only a matter of time before you got caught. So instead of owning up to it, you ran. Again."

Maddie's gaze bounced between them. "Will one of you please tell me what's going on?"

"Justin has been doing a little racing in his spare time." Just saying it out loud stoked the anger that had been simmering inside Aiden since he woke up in the hospital. He thought about the hours of painful rehab and the additional burden his injuries had placed on the family. "He was the one who ran me off the road that night."

Maddie blanched. "That can't be true..." She cast a beseeching look at Justin, waiting for him to deny it.

Aiden wanted Justin to deny it, too. But he didn't.

"It was an accident," he stammered. "He... I didn't mean to hurt anyone."

"Justin."

Maddie breathed the word, every emotion Aiden was feeling reflected in her eyes.

He steeled himself against the tear that traced a crooked path down Justin's cheek. "Even if that's true, you didn't even stop to make sure I was okay. You kept right on going."

"Hey." Another teenage boy stepped into the doorway—a younger version of Justin with the same slight build, brown hair and eyes. "What's going on?"

"Nothing." Justin's voice stretched thin. "We're just talking."

"Mom's working another shift, so I'm going over to Ryan's for a while."

"Not today," Justin snapped.

The boy's eyes widened. "Fine." The glower he cast at Aiden and Maddie showed he held them responsible for the change in his brother's attitude. "You—"

Whatever he'd been about to say was lost as Justin practically shoved him out of the shed.

When he turned back to Aiden, the tears had vanished and his shoulders were squared, as if a burden had been lifted.

"Go ahead and call the police. I know it's what you want to do."

Aiden shook his head. "You think I'm going to trust you'll stick around to give a statement? We're going to take a drive over to the sheriff's department together and have a chat with Deputy Bristow."

The shell-shocked look on Maddie's face was gone, but tears shimmered in her eyes, a reminder that Aiden wasn't the only one Justin had hurt. "I'll go with you."

"No." Aiden caught Maddie's hand, tempered his response by giving her fingers a reassuring squeeze. "I'll call you later," he promised.

"All right." She looked at Justin again, but the boy refused to meet her eyes.

The door closed, leaving them alone.

Aiden's knee was throbbing, but it didn't compare to the

crushing pain in his chest. He pointed to a paint-spattered wooden bench. "Sit down."

"Why?" Justin's chin jutted forward. "I thought we were going to have a chat with Deputy Bristow."

The kid really couldn't pull off defiant. He was a terrible liar, too.

"We are," Aiden said. "Right after you tell me the truth."

Maddie was spending the evening alternately praying and pacing when someone knocked on the door of her apartment.

She opened it, expecting to see her dad with a bag of groceries or a container of chocolate chip cookies, but it was Aiden who stood on the landing. Weary and disheveled and as handsome as the day they'd officially met.

"Hi, honey," he drawled. "How was your day?"

"Come inside." Maddie somehow managed to remember her recent decision to put some distance between her and Aiden. To force her hands to comply, to wave him into the living room, when what she really wanted to do was pull him into her arms.

His limp seemed more pronounced than usual, a sign he'd been on his feet too long. He bypassed the couch and lowered himself into her favorite chair.

Maddie would have offered him some of her emergency M&M's, but the bowl on the coffee table was empty.

Aiden leaned back. Flannel and faded denim should have looked comical against red velvet, but the dainty, embroidered cushions molded around Aiden's broad shoulders as if they'd been tailor-made for his frame.

"I'm sorry for coming over so late. I know I said I'd call, but I drove past and saw the lights on…"

"Don't apologize," Maddie said quickly. "I'm glad you stopped over. I wouldn't have slept a wink until I heard from you anyway."

She'd been on an emotional roller coaster since she'd left Justin's house. If the boy's confession had devastated Maddie, she could only imagine how Aiden felt.

"Carter let me sit in on the interview." Aiden's lips tipped in a wry smile. "It takes a lot longer than it does on TV."

Maddie saw the pain behind the smile. This time, she gave in to the impulse and reached for his hand. "Justin had us all fooled. I had no idea he was capable of something like this. Racing…it seems so out of character."

"It is," Aiden said. "That's why I knew he wasn't being honest with us."

Maddie stared at him. "What are you saying? That Justin *wasn't* driving the car that ran you off the road?"

"I'm saying he wasn't even in the car."

Maddie didn't bother trying to conceal her shock. "Then…who was?"

"His brother, Tim."

"The boy who came into the shed when we were talking to Justin today?" Justin had never mentioned a brother, but looking back, Maddie realized he didn't talk about his family at all.

Aiden nodded. "Tim turns sixteen in a few months. Justin has been helping him fix up their dad's old truck so he'd have something to drive when he got his license. Justin knew Tim had sneaked out and driven it a few times, but not that he'd buckled under pressure from some of his motorhead friends to prove it was as fast as he claimed it was.

"Justin had heard about my accident, but he thought the same thing everyone else did—that it was my fault. He didn't put two and two together until he overheard my conversation with Carter Bristow last Friday night. He confronted Tim when he got home."

"And he confessed?"

"Freaked out is probably more accurate. One of Tim's

friends was a passenger that night. They came around the corner too fast and crossed the center line." Aiden's expression darkened at the memory. "Both of them panicked when I took the ditch to avoid a head-on collision, but the friend looked back and claimed I'd steered back onto the road. I'm not sure if that was a lie or wishful thinking, but Tim believed him."

Now Maddie understood why Justin had dropped out of River Quest. The hero worship on the teenager's face was evident every time Aiden had coached them for the competition. The guilt that came from knowing his brother had been responsible for Aiden's injuries would have eaten Justin alive.

"If Tim is telling the truth and didn't know you'd been hurt, why did Justin take the blame?" That was something Maddie didn't understand. "Why didn't they go to the police and explain what had happened?"

"I asked Justin the same thing. Their dad walked out six months ago, and the kid definitely has some anger issues. Tim has been in trouble before, and leaving the scene of an accident you caused is a felony. Justin was scared to death Tim would get sent to a group home for repeat offenders."

"So Justin was protecting his brother," Maddie murmured.

"Yeah." Aiden slid a wry, sideways glance in her direction. "I don't get it myself."

Now who wasn't telling the truth? Even if there wasn't a hint of a smile in those cobalt-blue eyes, Maddie would have known that Aiden Kane, more than anyone, understood brotherly loyalty.

"After I got the truth out of Justin, I had a little talk with Tim and convinced him to talk to Deputy Bristow. The guy isn't Officer Friendly, but he's fair. Carter called Tim's caseworker at DHS, and I convinced them to let me sit in on the meeting, too. She agreed with me that it wouldn't be in Tim's best interests to prosecute him."

"The social worker agreed with you?"

"Ultimately, it's up to the judge, but I did tell the case-worker that we can always use some help in the shop if Tim needs a way to channel all that energy into something productive."

A lump instantly formed in Maddie's throat. Aiden had been so bitter the day they'd stumbled upon the damaged pickup. So set on holding the driver accountable for what he'd done.

What had changed in the last few hours?

She searched Aiden's face, and then she saw it. The peace she'd been praying he would find.

"It wasn't only for Tim, though, was it? You did it for Justin, too."

Aiden stared at Maddie in disbelief.

How did she *know* that? Did librarians have some special superpower, some kind of mysterious intuition that told them when there was more to the story?

"Justin?" Aiden should have known better than to play dumb with a woman as intelligent as Maddie.

"You knew what it would do to Justin if he was separated from his brother," she said softly. "He would have blamed himself."

"He already does." Aiden tipped his head toward the ceiling. "After Justin's dad left, his mom took another job to pay the bills. When Tim got in trouble the first time, she told Justin he had to keep a closer eye on him."

"Tim isn't a toddler," Maddie protested. "It wasn't Justin's fault."

"That's not the way he saw it."

You won't understand.

Justin had hurled the words at Aiden after he'd told

him what had happened the night of the accident, the tears flowing hard and fast from his eyes.

"I knew Tim was sneaking out of the house and I didn't say anything," he'd said. "Mom had said if he gets into any more trouble he'll either go to the group home or foster care. If that happens, it will be my fault."

My fault. My fault. My fault.

The words had ricocheted through Aiden's head. Drained away his anger in a single exhale.

He'd asked Justin for the truth, not knowing it would shine a light on all the lies that had attached themselves to his heart and weighed it down.

"Justin didn't realize we have something in common. Every time my brothers and I were placed in temporary foster care, Mom made sure I knew it was my fault. She said I made her look like a bad parent because I was out of control." He sighed, gathering strength. "I was never forgiven for making mistakes. In fact, I figured out pretty quick that I *was* the mistake. I kept trying to do better. *Be* better." Aiden had lost count of the number of times he'd tried to work his way into his parents' favor. "I thought I'd left all that junk at the foot of the cross when I gave my life to God. I didn't realize I'd just gotten used to carrying it. And then..."

"The accident?" Maddie didn't pull her hand away. Her fingers notched with his, small and delicate, and yet somehow they made Aiden feel stronger. Strong enough to tell her the truth.

"It was before that," Aiden admitted. "I told Justin I knew all about guilt because I'm the reason Mom put our baby sister up for adoption."

"Aiden..." Maddie breathed. "You don't know that."

"It's okay. I realized that all the things I said to Justin... those are the things God has been trying to tell me. I can't earn His love or work my way into the family, because I'm already His son."

And finding their sister had become another way Aiden had tried to prove his worth to the family. Prove he belonged.

"It was Justin's expression when I told him I understood that blew me away. He expected me to ask Deputy Bristow to lock him and Tim up and throw away the key because that's what he thought he deserved. Grace, not so much. I decided if I was going to encourage Justin to put his trust in God, I should be doing the same thing. So I asked him to give me the right words."

"And He did?" Maddie asked the question, but the smile on her face told Aiden she already knew the answer.

"In a roundabout way." He loved Maddie's smile. "I told him that God can bring something good out of this because *He's* good."

Astonishment filled Maddie's eyes when she realized he'd quoted her.

Aiden's cell phone buzzed, signaling an incoming text. He glanced at the message from Tyler.

Flamethrowers back in the race

He grinned and held it up for Maddie to read.

"See what I mean?"

Chapter Eighteen

"I can't decide, Maddie." Courtney Meade held up two of the historical romance novels she loved to read. "Which one would you recommend?"

"The beauty of our annual sale is that you don't have to choose," Maddie pointed out with a smile. "You can buy both with a clear conscience because all the proceeds go toward our Bountiful Books campaign."

"You're right." Courtney returned Maddie's smile with a sly wink, grabbed two more titles and fanned them out in front of her. "It is important to support a worthy cause."

Like the community's fall festival, the library's book drive had become an annual event. Every November, Maddie put an enormous wicker cornucopia in the window of the library. People in the community and local business owners would fill it with books, and then a special guest would hand them out to children before the tree lighting ceremony the first weekend in December. Maddie was still hoping the author of the Winter series would agree to attend, but so far, there'd been no response to her email.

She reached down to get a paper sack, and a shadow fell across the table, blotting out the sun. Maddie glanced up, and her heart took a swan dive all the way down to her toes.

Aiden. And in a River Quest T-shirt and charcoal-gray

cargo pants, he looked better than the trays of apple cider doughnuts for sale in the next booth over.

He looked a little frustrated, too, which set off warning bells in Maddie's head.

"Aiden…the race starts in an hour. What are you doing here?"

"What are *you* doing here?" he countered.

Maddie blinked. Wasn't it obvious? She was doing what she did every year during the fall festival. "Supervising the used book sale?"

"I can see that," Aiden muttered. "But you're the Flamethrowers' sponsor. I thought you'd want to be there to cheer the team on."

"Skye has everything under control, and the boys seemed fine when I talked to them last night." Maddie stammered. "I didn't think they needed me."

"I—of course they need you." Aiden scowled. "Skye sprayed red streaks in her hair—she brought extra for you, by the way—and Tyler's parents are planning to come. His mom took the weekend off so Ty's dad could watch him compete."

"That's wonderful."

Thank you, Lord.

From the moment her feet had touched the floor that morning, Maddie had been praying for Tyler and Justin. Praying for Aiden.

River Quest was important to all of them, albeit for very different reasons.

"I'd better stop by and see what all the excitement is about," Courtney interjected, batting her eyelashes flirtatiously at Aiden and reminding Maddie they weren't alone.

Such was the effect Aiden Kane had on her. He made her forget all kinds of things. Like why spending more time with him, being near him, would only make it more difficult to go back to her normal life when the festival was over.

"Enjoy the rest of the weekend, Courtney." Maddie slipped a bookmark into the bag. "And thank you for your donation!"

The moment the woman stepped away from the table, Aiden took her place. "Ready?"

"I can't just abandon the booth," Maddie protested. "Proceeds from the sale go toward a special book drive next month."

"So you can't leave until they're gone."

Now he understood. "Exactly."

"Fine. I'll take all of them."

"All…" Maddie choked.

"Yup." Aiden extracted his wallet. "What do I owe you?"

"It's by donation," someone called.

Courtney had drifted away, but Maddie suddenly realized they still had an audience. The people who'd been milling around Olivia Thorne's stand must have decided the café owner's apple cider doughnuts weren't nearly as interesting as the conversation taking place by the used book sale and drifted closer.

"Great." Aiden tucked a fifty-dollar bill through the opening in the canister Maddie had set out on the table. "I'll see you in fifteen minutes."

"Look out!" Skye called cheerfully. "Low-flying branch!"

"Thanks." Maddie ducked underneath it. She'd dressed for a day in the book sale booth, not trekking through the woods, but at least she'd had her hiking boots in the back seat of the car. Her bun had begun to disintegrate before the fourth challenge, so she'd threaded her hair through the keyhole of the Castle Falls Outfitters ball cap that Lily had plunked on her head. The bright red T-shirt Skye had designed for the team, knotted at the waist of Maddie's knee-length cotton sundress, completed her fashion ensemble.

"Do you think we're ahead of them?" Skye hopped over a fallen log. "I want to get a few more close-ups."

Maddie hoped so, but the last time they'd caught a glimpse of the boys, Justin and Tyler had been maneuvering their canoe through The Serpent's Tail. Tyler, soaking wet and grinning from ear to ear, had spotted them on shore and raised his paddle in the air. A charming salute Skye had captured on video.

Maddie hadn't seen Aiden since the start of the competition.

Joy and thankfulness welled up inside her when he'd walked to the center of the makeshift stage by the river.

Aiden wasn't able to accompany his brothers from checkpoint to checkpoint, but he'd been the perfect MC, opening with a story meant to build the spectators' excitement and cracking jokes to ease the competitors' anxiety.

Watching Aiden flash that thousand-kilowatt smile, it was easy to see why the crowd loved him. Maddie couldn't have been more proud of the man…until Aiden had dedicated the race to Rich Mason. And read the verse in Psalm One that had inspired the Castle Falls Outfitters logo, a tree that reflected the family's deep faith as well as the business.

She'd lost sight of Aiden after that. She and Skye had decided to make their way over to The Pendulum and wait there until the boys showed up.

It was a good thing, too. The map had laid out the course but not the terrain around it, and they were on foot, not driving Aiden's UTV. While other spectators had made their way to the scenic picnic routes positioned along the way, Skye wanted to get close-up shots of Tyler and Justin. And in order to accomplish that, she and Maddie had to move from obstacle to obstacle.

"The next challenge should be right around this cor—" Skye skidded to a stop with a low groan, and Maddie had to do a quick sidestep into the brush to avoid bumping into her. "Seriously? Aiden couldn't have put that thing at the beginning of the race when people still had some energy?"

Maddie followed the girl's gaze and silently agreed.

A net fashioned from heavy rope, taller than the wall they'd built for The Pendulum, crisscrossed between two massive white pines like an enormous spiderweb.

"The boys can do it, right?" Skye looked to Maddie for affirmation.

"Of course." If they made it this far. A canoe sporting bright red flames had been noticeably absent in the last group Maddie had watched glide down the river, and she was getting a little concerned.

Justin and Tyler had had an amazing instructor, but they were still novices, not seasoned outdoorsmen.

What if something unexpected had happened? What if they'd capsized? Run aground?

A shout drew her attention to a narrow opening in the trees.

"There they are!" Skye got so excited when Tyler and Justin sprinted toward them that she forgot to record the moment and waved the camera over her head instead. "Come on! You're almost there!"

Justin flashed a thumbs-up as they reached the web, but instead of beginning the climb, the boys skidded to a stop right at the bottom.

Tyler folded over in a bow and swept out his arm. "Ladies first!"

Skye didn't have to be asked twice. She grabbed Maddie's hand. "Let's do it!"

A surge of adrenaline had Maddie's heart beating in double time as she looked up—*and up*—at the obstacle Aiden had appropriately dubbed The Black Widow.

"You go, Skye," she urged. "If the guys wait for me, I'll mess up their time."

"Oh, no." Tyler shook his head. "There are a few teams behind us, and the finish line is only a quarter mile away—"

"So we're all going." Justin folded his arms over his chest.

"Come on, Miss M!" Skye was already reaching for the rope.

A loud shout from a rival team racing toward the wall forced Maddie to make a decision. She grabbed the rope and followed Skye.

Halfway up, the net heaved as the other team began their ascent. Maddie's foot slipped off the rope, and she made the mistake of looking down.

The ground appeared to be a lot farther away than when she'd been standing on it.

A hand closed around Maddie's ankle.

"You can do it, Miss M." Justin grinned up at her. "The only person who doesn't finish is the one who gives up."

A fresh surge of adrenaline surged through Maddie. It wasn't the inspirational quote that inspired Maddie to keep going, though. Justin's grin was worth more than one of the trophies lined up on the victory platform.

She found her footing and pulled herself up and over the top of the wall.

Maddie's muscles burned, the pressure in her chest a reminder that she spent her days walking between walls of books, not climbing ones made of rope.

All four of them hit the ground running. It didn't even occur to Maddie to let the boys go on ahead without her.

She loped along beside Skye, grateful that Aiden had integrated an old corduroy logging road into the last leg of the journey. After climbing the rope wall, he must have realized the competitors would need a break.

The course ran parallel with the river, and then looped

back through the woods to the original starting point so spectators could cheer the teams on as they made their way to the finish line.

"I smell smoke," Skye panted.

"The last challenge!" Justin called over his shoulder. "It's the ring of fire."

"The torches aren't in a circle, though." Tyler dropped back to give more instructions. "It's a maze. Aiden couldn't tell us which way to go, so we'll have to figure it out when we get there."

Maddie was tempted to break from the rest of the team and head straight for the woods. She'd seen the words *fire ring* on the map, of course, but assumed it was a campfire. The friendly kind people gathered around.

No one had said anything about running *through* it.

"Teams five and six coming in," Liam announced.

Aiden stepped closer to the edge of the platform, but all he could see were four shadowy figures moving through the smoke.

The spectators gathered on the lawn began to applaud. Amazingly enough, the size of the crowd had only increased as the afternoon wore on, thanks to his family. Some of the visitors lingered in the yard, sampling the ice-cream sundaes that Anna's mother, Nancy, had been dishing out to raise money for the animal shelter. Others wandered through the Trading Post, shopping for treasures.

The number of people who'd turned out for the event had surpassed Aiden's expectations, but after watching Tyler and Justin launch his canoe in the river, he realized he wasn't interested in numbers anymore.

Aiden wasn't sure quite when that had happened—but he knew who was responsible.

A petite, green-eyed librarian had changed Aiden's definition of success.

Changed *him.*

Because of Maddie, Aiden had called his first family meeting in the history of Kane family meetings. He hadn't known quite where to start, so he'd followed Maddie's lead and started with prayer. Being honest with God, Aiden had discovered, had made it easier to be honest with Sunni and his brothers.

He'd told them about Justin and the part Tim had played in the accident. His doubts about God and his value in the family.

Brendan and Liam hadn't said a word, but the stunned expressions on their faces told Aiden he'd been wrong about that, too.

"It's not two teams. They're all wearing red shirts." Tim, Justin's brother, had pinched Aiden's binoculars. Along with Tyler's parents, the boy had been given VIP privileges: courtside seats on the victory platform and all the lemonade they could drink.

"Red?" Aiden reached for the binoculars as the foursome burst through the wall of smoke.

Liam leaned forward. "Is that..."

"Maddie."

Aiden couldn't believe it, either, but there she was, zigzagging through the maze of torches that led to the finish line.

Chapter Nineteen

Pride and fear battled for dominance as Aiden watched Maddie keep pace with Skye while the boys charged ahead of them toward the platform.

"Sorry, folks!" Liam grinned down at the people crowded around the platform. "I was wrong. Fifth place in today's competition is the Flamethrowers."

From the commotion on the stage, Aiden would have thought that Tyler and Justin had been in first place. To his chagrin, most of it came from his own family, who swarmed up the steps to offer their congratulations.

Sunni had taken the Owens family under her wing the moment they'd arrived, handing Tyler's mom, Sandie, a glass of lemonade and his father, Kenny, a thin, spindly-legged puppy, one of the animal shelter's new arrivals.

"Murphy is a little nervous around strangers," Sunni had whispered. "Do you mind holding him for a few minutes?"

Aiden had no doubt the "few minutes" would turn into hours, and Tyler's dad would go home with a new companion.

"We're going to do this next year," Tyler had promised his dad.

Kenny Owens looked pleased. He nodded at Justin. "Looks to me like you've already got a teammate."

Tyler nudged his friend. "He's ditching me to go to college, isn't that right, Einstein?"

"Right." Justin glanced down at the man's wheelchair, and Aiden could practically see him working on modifications so people with physical disabilities could take part in the competition.

"Pssst." Liam pressed the microphone into Aiden's hand. "You're supposed to be congratulating the team, not ogling their sponsor," he whispered.

Aiden had been *admiring*, not ogling, but there was no time to set his brother straight.

The rest of the competitors arrived in quick succession, forcing Aiden to concentrate on his duties as MC. By the time the closing ceremony ended, Maddie was nowhere in sight.

Aiden plucked a bottle of water from the cooler on the end of the stage and set out across the yard.

"If you're looking for Maddie," Rebecca Tamblin called out, "I saw her over by the Trading Post, talking to Anna."

Aiden didn't deny it. Just like he wasn't going to deny that his feelings for Maddie had changed over the past few weeks.

Sure, he hadn't seen her since the night he'd shown up at her apartment with the news about Justin, but Maddie was committed to her job. She'd mentioned the used book sale was part of a larger fund-raiser, so it made sense that the week leading up to the fall festival would require a lot of her time.

Now that it was over, though—leaving Aiden set for Christmas and birthday gifts for years to come—he had other plans that would take up Maddie's free time.

Long walks in the woods. Watching the night sky.

Kissing her under the stars with no interruptions—

"Uncle Aiden! Come and see the puppies!" Cassie and Chloe intercepted him halfway to the house.

"Hey, copper tops." He went down on his good knee and opened his arms.

The twins hung back.

"Mommy said we can't hug you because your ribs hurt," Chloe told him.

"Is that so?" Aiden cocked an eyebrow. "Because I happen to think that hugs make a person heal *faster*. Should we test the theory and see if I'm right?"

"Okay!" The twins snuggled close, cheeks pressed against Aiden's chest, tickling his nose with the scent of sunscreen and strawberry shampoo.

Man, Liam was blessed. For weeks, Aiden had been teasing his big brother about losing his heart, but now he understood that *losing* was entirely the wrong word.

It was more about finding, really. And when a man found someone like Anna—or Maddie—he didn't lose his heart. He gave it away. Freely. Without reservation.

"I'll come over in a few minutes to see those puppies," Aiden promised the girls. "But I have to talk to Maddie first."

"She's over there." Cassie pointed over his shoulder.

Over the tops of their heads, Aiden spotted a slight figure in the distance. But Maddie wasn't talking to the twins' mother outside the Trading Post.

She was walking toward her car.

"Hey." Aiden caught up to Maddie and slid into the passenger side of her car. "I thought you'd stick around a while."

Maddie turned the key in the ignition. "I have to change clothes."

Aiden thought she looked beautiful.

"All the competitors got one of these, and the Flamethrowers wanted to make sure you did, too."

Maddie looked down at the pin cradled in his palm. "Those were for the teams who finished the race."

"Exactly." Aiden bent closer and carefully attached the tiny copper tree to the front of Maddie's ball cap. Her hair flowed out the back in a long ponytail, and he couldn't resist toying with one of the "flames" that Skye had painted in her hair. "I like the new look, by the way."

"Skye promised it will wash out after the sixth shampoo."

Maddie shifted, putting some space between them, and Aiden's hand fell away.

For the first time, he noticed the pallor under Maddie's sun-kissed cheeks, and the beads of moisture glistening on her forehead.

"You overdid it today, didn't you?" Aiden had been so proud when she'd burst through the wall of smoke, it hadn't occurred to him she shouldn't have been running in the first place.

"I—" Maddie moistened her bottom lip with her tongue. "I got caught up in the moment but it's… I'm fine."

She didn't *look* fine, but Aiden knew the perfect way to relax.

"Sunni is one of the judges for the chili cook-off tonight, so the family is guaranteed a spot in the pavilion," he said. "There's going to be a folk band, too."

"It's Saturday." Maddie fidgeted with the keys. "My parents are expecting me for supper."

Maddie. Fidgeting. Now Aiden knew something was wrong.

"Tell your mom she can get a break from cooking and invite them to come with us instead."

"Aiden…" Something in the way she said his name instantly triggered a feeling of dread. "That isn't a good idea."

"Sure it is. I know you said that your parents are a little protective, but don't worry. I'll win them over with my dashing good looks and rapier wit."

"Aiden." Maddie's gaze lit on him for a moment, and in

spite of the unseasonably warm October afternoon, he went cold all over. "None of this is a good idea. River Quest is over now and we…*we* aren't going to work."

Had he misread the hum of electricity in the air whenever they were together? The way her eyelashes had drifted shut, the way she'd leaned into him, in the library when they'd almost kissed?

"You're saying you don't feel anything for me other than friendship?"

"There's a…spark, yes," she said carefully. "But that isn't enough to build a relationship on. You have to admit we…we really don't have anything in common. Now that you're moving around better, you'll spend time doing the things you loved before the accident, and so will I."

He loved spending time with Maddie, but apparently she didn't feel the same way.

Idiot, Aiden inwardly chided himself.

"I'll keep looking for your sister, though," Maddie continued, no longer looking him in the eye. "And I'll let you know right away if I find something."

Because helping people in the community was part of her job. Aiden's mistake was letting himself believe that he'd become more than a work project.

"Don't worry about it." Aiden resisted the urge to snap the way Dodger did in an attempt to let out some of the pain. "I'll take it from here."

It would have hurt less if Maddie had just reached in and pulled his heart right out of his chest.

Hadn't it been clear from the start that he wasn't in her league?

Aiden had bared his soul, revealed his flaws, and Maddie obviously hadn't liked what she'd seen. Now she was attempting to let him down easy with the classic "it's not you, it's me" speech when they both knew the truth.

It was him.

* * *

Maddie bumped open the screen door with her shoulder and winced. The muscles she'd pushed earlier that day were pushing back. A hot bath would take away the ache in her limbs, but nothing would ease the weight pressing down on her shoulders.

She'd done it. Told Aiden there was no point in taking their friendship to the next level.

Managed to hold back the tears until he'd walked away.

She could hear classical music drifting from the living room and poked her head around the corner. Her parents sat on the couch, separated only by the enormous bowl of popcorn they were sharing, watching Ginger Rogers and Fred Astaire dance in the rain.

"I'm sorry I'm late." Maddie deposited the plate of cookies she'd bought from the bake sale on the table. "I had to put a few things away before I left."

"Maddie." Her mom bounced off the couch so fast the bowl of popcorn almost came with her. "We didn't think you'd be coming over tonight."

"It's Saturday."

Her parents exchanged a sideways glance.

"Yes…but we thought you'd be going to the chili cook-off," her dad said.

The words *chili cook-off* should not have created a lump the size of a golf ball in Maddie's throat. "I never have before."

And now that River Quest was over, things would go on exactly as before.

The lump got bigger.

"Sweetheart, can you pause the movie for a minute? I'm sure Maddie is hungry." Tara ushered Maddie into the kitchen. "Your dad and I ate a little while ago, but there's chicken salad in the refrigerator."

The thought of food made Maddie's stomach pitch, but

she'd come over for supper, so turning down food would raise questions Maddie didn't want to answer.

She pulled the salad out of the fridge and caught her mom staring.

"The dye will wash out." Maddie fingered one of the red streaks in her hair and inadvertently allowed a memory to sneak in.

I like the new look, Aiden had said.

But the dye, like the time she'd spent with Aiden, was temporary. Maddie had to think about the future.

"I was looking at your pin," her mom said. "Is that one of Anna Leighton's designs?"

Maddie reached up and touched the tiny copper tree pinned to her hat. "Aid—" She caught herself before saying his name. "Castle Falls Outfitters gave them out to the teams that finished the race. Justin and Tyler thought I should have one, too, because I was the team sponsor."

"I don't think your being the sponsor had anything to do with it, Maddie. From what I've heard, those three teenagers obviously love you. And—" her mom slanted a knowing look in Maddie's direction "—it appears that someone else does, too."

Unbelievable. People were talking about *her*?

"Aiden and I…it would never work, Mom. We're too different. He loves to push himself. Take risks."

"And running through a maze of burning torches isn't risky?"

Maddie winced.

Her mom had heard about that, too?

"I didn't overdo it," Maddie said quickly, attempting to circumvent the gentle lecture she knew was coming before it began. "I know what I can and can't do."

Although there'd been times over the past month when the line between the two had become blurred.

"I know you do, sweetheart. And I'm sorry."

"For what?"

"Your dad and I…we were terrified of losing you. After the surgeries, we were determined to do everything we could to keep you happy and healthy." Tara hooked a tendril of crimson hair behind Maddie's ear. "But I'm afraid that somewhere along the way, we didn't put as much emphasis on the happy part."

"I'm happy," Maddie protested.

"I know you are," Tara said softly. "But I've seen a difference in you the past few weeks, and this math teacher hasn't been retired so long that she can't spot the new variable in the equation." Her mom was smiling now. "If God has brought a man into your life who makes you laugh, makes that wonderful heart of yours beat a little faster, I would tell you, Madeline Rose, to take the risk. Love is worth it."

"I don't—" *Love Aiden*, Maddie was about to say before a line from Jane Austen's *Emma* ran through her head.

Then I examined my own heart. And there you were. Never, I fear, to be removed.

But didn't loving someone mean putting their needs first?

Maddie was being honest when she'd told Aiden that she'd gotten caught up in the moment. For a few glorious days, Maddie had actually let herself dream about a future with him.

And then she'd seen the expression on Aiden's face earlier that afternoon when Anna's twins ran up to him. Tenderness. Longing.

After his tumultuous childhood, it was no wonder that Aiden wanted—*deserved*—a family of his own.

A family Maddie couldn't give him.

Chapter Twenty

Aiden shuffled up the stairs—without the aid of his crutch *or* the wooden handrail.

He was free. The physical therapist and his doctor had both given Aiden permission to resume his day-to-day activities as long as he didn't overdo it, an announcement that should have had him celebrating the return to his normal life.

Except for the fact that he was miserable, because Maddie was no longer part of it.

"It's not Maddie's fault." Aiden had reached that conclusion the moment her car had disappeared from sight. "It's mine."

Behind him, he heard a growl of agreement.

Aiden glanced at Dodger. "One, I didn't ask for your opinion. And two, if you keep up the attitude, there's an empty kennel at the shelter with your name on it."

Dodger stared at him, bushy eyebrows rising a fraction of an inch. *You're bluffing*, they said.

If Aiden didn't know better, he'd think the dog had actually understood the conversation Aiden had had with Sunni the week before.

She'd swept into the sunroom, a handful of dog biscuits in one hand and a snazzy matching collar and leash in the other.

"Does Dodger have another vet appointment?" Aiden had asked.

"Not today" came the cheerful reply. "Dr. Voss called this morning, and based on Dodger's latest examination, he's been cleared for active duty. There's room at the shelter, so I think it's time I find this guy a forever home. There's a new family at church interested in adopting an older dog."

"A family?" Aiden had frowned. "With little kids?"

"Dodger has never shown any sign of aggression toward the twins," Sunni pointed out. "Or other animals, for that matter."

"What about all the snapping and snarling?"

"*He* hasn't done any of that for the past few weeks." His mom had emphasized the first word. "Animals, like people, react out of their pain, you know."

Aiden *did* know, but he wasn't going there. His family hadn't asked about Maddie since the fall festival, but he'd caught their speculative looks. Probably wondering what he'd done to mess things up this time.

"I don't think Dodger is going to adjust well to being moved around. They could come over here so I—" Aiden caught himself. "*They* can meet him."

After Sunni left, Aiden had found the collar and leash on the table with his cell phone number engraved on the silver tag.

"Come on." He glanced down at the dog. Dodger wasn't moving as fast as Aiden, but he was just as determined to conquer the stairs. "If I can do it, so can you."

Aiden paused on the landing and gave the doorknob an experimental turn with his injured wrist. All he felt was a mild tweak of discomfort instead of pain.

Dodger bounded—*bounded!*—across the room and launched himself onto the sofa.

"Make yourself at home," Aiden said drily.

Sunlight flooded the room, and it was obvious the women in the family had been there ahead of him. The smell of freshly baked bread permeated the room. The floor gleamed from its recent scrubbing, and a bouquet of yellow mums, the last holdouts from Sunni's garden, sat on the coffee table.

Liam's duffel bag and a tower of cardboard boxes marked another change. Dodger was moving in, and by the end of the day, his brother would be moved out.

The major work on the cabin had been completed, and Liam had decided it would be easier to put on the finishing touches if he lived on-site.

"You'll finally have the place to yourself," Liam had teased Aiden after breaking the news. "You won't have to speed up the process by putting pinecones in my boots or short-sheeting my bed."

Maybe not, but Aiden was going to miss his brother's reaction—and his company.

Footsteps in the stairwell told Aiden that the time was at hand.

"Are you in that much of a hurry—" The breath poured out of Aiden's lungs in a soft whoosh.

Maddie stood on the landing. Her hair was in a loose braid over one shoulder. A rose-colored dress skimmed her slender curves and flared out several inches above the ruffled socks peeking over the tops of suede…hiking boots.

After two weeks of having to get used to Maddie's absence the way he'd had to get used to the weakness in his limbs, she was here.

Sweet and beautiful and *here.*

"I… Can we talk?"

Was she kidding? Aiden had been praying he'd hear those words.

"Sure." He motioned to the sofa, and Dodger curled up in a ball to make room, the thump of his tail against the cushion matching the beat of Aiden's heart. "Come in."

But Maddie, instead of stepping into the room, took a step backward. The guarded expression on her face instantly doused the hope that had kindled inside Aiden, like a cold rain might.

"It's about your sister."

"Then my family is going to want to hear it, too?"

"Yes."

"All right. Let's go find them."

Aiden had a few moments to brace himself for whatever news had brought Maddie here. And the knowledge that once she'd said it, she'd be walking out of his life again.

Lord, I need your help.

Maddie sent up the silent prayer as Aiden followed her down the stairs. He kept pace with her now, his stride smooth and confident, no longer hampered by his injuries.

She'd known it would be difficult to see Aiden again, but the speech Maddie had prepared dissolved the moment their eyes met.

How had it happened that a man she'd met a month ago had taken up so much space in her heart?

"Everyone is watching football." Aiden opened the door and let Maddie go in first.

Keeping the family's Sunday afternoon pizza tradition in mind, Maddie had chosen today on purpose, hoping the entire family would be in attendance.

Laughter drifted down the hallway, and Maddie almost lost her nerve as she stepped through the doorway into the living room.

Sunni sat in the rocking chair, a puff of a gray kitten

curled up in her lap. Liam and Anna cuddled together at one end of the sectional sofa. Brendan and Lily sat on the opposite side, and Cassie and Chloe sprawled on the floor near their feet playing tug-of-war with Missy.

Cassie spotted her first. "Miss Maddie!"

Everyone's attention shifted from the game, and they immediately made room, as if Maddie belonged there.

Her mouth turned as dry as sawdust, and Aiden came to her rescue.

"Can we take a break from the game and talk for a few minutes?"

"You're calling another family meeting?" Brendan teased.

"Actually, it was Maddie's idea."

The television screen went blank, and Lily hopped to her feet. "Girls, how about you take Missy outside to play for a few minutes?"

"Okay, Aunt Lily!"

They skipped past Maddie, and no one said anything until the front door snapped shut.

"Would you like to sit down, Maddie?" Sunni was already pouring a glass of lemonade from a pitcher on the end table.

Maddie nodded and sank gratefully into a wide-lapped tweed chair, not trusting her knees would hold her up much longer.

"Aiden told you that I was helping him find your sister." Maddie's gaze lit briefly on Liam and Brendan before moving to Lily. "The weekend before the fall festival, you talked about your friend Shelby. You said you'd grown up together and that you told each other everything."

Lily nodded, prompting Maddie to continue with an encouraging smile.

"Aiden had mentioned there was a woman… Trish Jenkins, who'd contacted you when your…when Carla died. I thought that maybe, if she'd confided in Trish about her sons…maybe she'd confided in her about her daughter, too. So instead of looking for the agency who'd handled the adoption, I started looking for Trish instead." Maddie swallowed hard. "And… I found her."

No one moved. The silence that followed seemed to steal the oxygen from the room.

Brendan was the first person to speak. "Did you talk to her? Does she know what happened to our sister?"

Maddie didn't realize she'd knotted her fingers together in her lap until Sunni's hand folded over hers. Gave it a gentle squeeze.

"We spoke on the phone last night. Trish didn't want to tell me anything at first, because Carla had sworn her to secrecy." Maddie's eyes met Aiden's across the room. "I'm sorry. I'm not trying to be dramatic…it's just hard for me to tell you this."

"It's okay, Maddie," Liam said quietly. "No matter what you found out, it's better than not knowing."

"Our biological parents had a pretty dysfunctional relationship," Brendan added. "We won't be shocked if you tell us that our mom was unfaithful. Even if we have a half sister, she's still family."

"She's not your half sister." Tears scalded the backs of Maddie's eyes. "Your mom found out she was expecting a few months after they separated for the first time."

"So our timeline was off?" Aiden spoke for the first time since Anna's girls had left the room.

Maddie drew in a breath. Not only the timeline. The whole circumstances surrounding their sister's birth.

"According to Trish, Carla gave birth to twins."

The people in the room looked shell-shocked. It was the same reaction Maddie had experienced when she'd heard the word.

"She gave *two* babies up for adoption?" Aiden choked out, pushing off from the wall.

The butterflies that had taken up residence in Maddie's stomach tried to beat their way out. "Not two." She looked at Aiden. "Carla brought you home."

"Me?" Aiden choked out. "You're saying that I have a *twin* sister?"

Maddie bit her lip. Nodded. "There were complications after she was born, and she spent another month in the NICU. While she was there, one of the volunteers who came in and rocked babies fell in love with her. Trish wasn't sure how it happened, but your mom granted the woman and her husband temporary custody of the baby when she was released from the hospital."

"But the conversation I overheard between Carla and the caseworker..." Brendan looked incredulous. "Aiden was five years old."

"So was your sister." Maddie closed her eyes briefly, and Aiden knew she wasn't gathering her thoughts. She was praying. "According to Trish, Carla had always intended to bring her home. But the more time that went by, the more she struggled over separating the baby from the only parents she'd ever known. Carla told Trish she'd decided to terminate her rights because she didn't want her daughter to grow up without choices, the way she had. She wanted her to have a different kind of life."

Aiden felt the ripples of another aftershock sweep through his body.

All this time Aiden had believed it was his fault that Carla had put their baby sister up for adoption. But if what Trish had told Maddie was true, the woman who'd claimed she'd never wanted to be a mother had, for the first time, acted like one. She'd put her daughter's needs above her own.

"What else can you tell us about her?" Lily clung to Brendan's arm. "Do you know her name? Where she's living now?"

"Trish doesn't know your sister's name or the name of the family who adopted her," Maddie said. "But she did remember the name of the private adoption agency. Holt-McIntyre. I… I actually spoke with one of the caseworkers a few weeks ago."

A few weeks ago? And she hadn't said anything?

As if Maddie read his mind, she cast him a beseeching glance. "Victoria Gerard called in response to an email I'd sent, but it sounds like they adhere to a strict set of rules."

"A closed adoption through a private agency." Aiden's back teeth ground together. "So that takes us right back to square one."

"Victoria did say if there were unique circumstances, the board might agree to look over a petition and 'determine whether there's cause to contact the adoptee.'"

"Unique." Liam raked his hand through his hair. "I'd say that describes the circumstances, all right."

Brendan nodded. "So we file a petition."

Aiden was glad his brothers were thinking clearly because he wasn't.

Not only did he have a sister, he had a *twin*.

Aiden walked over to the window on legs that weren't quite steady.

"We're going to find her." Liam and Brendan moved, too. Positioned themselves around Aiden like two offensive linemen protecting their quarterback.

Yes, they were. Thanks to Maddie, who'd continued the search even though he'd asked her not to.

Except he hadn't thanked her yet, had he?

Aiden's gaze landed on an empty chair. Maddie had slipped away while his back was turned.

They were one step closer to finding their sister, and yet Aiden couldn't shake an overwhelming sense of loss.

"What are you doing?"

Brendan's voice—accompanied by a cuff to the shoulder—yanked Aiden's attention away from the chair.

"I…nothing."

"That's obvious," Liam said drily. "But the bigger question is *why*."

The three women closed in around him, obviously as interested in his answer as his annoying older brothers.

"Because I'm still trying to wrap my head around the fact I have a twin sister." Trying to wrap his head around the fact that Maddie had delivered the news and walked away without a backward glance. At least she'd said goodbye the last time.

"Let me rephrase that." Liam, the brother known for his patience, looked like he wanted to cuff Aiden on the shoulder, too. "Why aren't you going after Maddie?"

They were going to make him say it.

"This wasn't a social call. I'd asked Maddie to help me find our sister, and that's what she did. She isn't interested in me…not like that."

Aiden hadn't expected his brothers to wrap him in a group hug, but he hadn't expected them to burst out laughing, either.

"Not interested in you?" Sunni echoed. "That young woman happens to be crazy about you."

"You're my mom," Aiden said patiently. "It's your job to think every single woman in Castle Falls is crazy about me."

"Of course it is." Sunni folded her arms. "But in this case, I happen to be right."

Aiden appreciated the family's loyalty, but Maddie hadn't made any effort to contact him until now. If it was true that actions spoke louder than words, then Maddie had made her feelings crystal clear.

"I asked Maddie out, she turned me down, end of story." Aiden tempered the words with a smile. "Now, if you'll excuse me, I have a date with a canoe."

Even though he had a feeling that thoughts of Maddie would follow him down the river, too.

"Aiden? Can I talk to you for a minute?"

Anna was the last person Aiden had expected to follow him out the door. If it would have been one of his brothers, he might have kept going, but it was impossible to ignore a request from his gentle future sister-in-law.

"Sure."

To his surprise, Anna gestured toward Brendan's office at the far end of the hall, a room that would ensure some privacy.

"I appreciate your support, Anna," Aiden said the moment they were alone. "But as far as Maddie and I are concerned, there's really nothing to talk about."

Because there was no "him and Maddie" at all.

"All right." Anna released a slow breath. "Do you mind if we talk about me, then?"

"Um..." The question threw him off for a moment. Had he misunderstood Anna's reason for wanting to talk to him? "No. Of course not."

"I don't know if Liam told you anything about my marriage to Ross, but it wasn't good." Anna's golden-brown eyes clouded. "Everyone in Castle Falls thought we'd had this storybook romance, but he was...abusive. Until God brought Liam into my life, I didn't realize how many walls I'd put around my heart."

Liam had never shared that piece of Anna's past with him. The thought of Ross Leighton treating Anna that way had Aiden's hands curling into fists at his side. "You can trust my brother. Our dad was a piece of work, but Liam... he'd never hurt you."

"Trusting *was* hard for me," Anna said candidly. "But Liam didn't give up."

"That's because he's Liam. He's one of the good guys."

"So are you."

When Aiden didn't respond, Anna set her hands on her hips, and the stern look she leveled at Aiden made him feel like he was the twins' age.

"You took those teenagers under your wing and helped their families in the process. I may be new to the family, but I've seen how Liam—and Brendan—depend on you."

"For comic relief, maybe."

"For inspiration. You're like Joshua. You're not reckless, you're brave. You remind people that our faith journey is an adventure. A lack of fear isn't always foolishness, you know. Sometimes it's trusting in a God who can do the impossible."

Aiden stared at her, speechless. Joshua happened to be one of his Old Testament heroes.

"Maddie might have said you don't have anything in common, but that's not true," Anna continued. "You both have a strong faith. You love your families and show compassion to people no one else seems to notice. Those are the things that are really important. There's also a fair amount of chemistry, from what I could see." Anna's lips twitched. "I can tell when a woman is in love, Aiden. Maddie couldn't take her eyes off you when you walked onto the stage before River Quest."

"And then a few hours later she said she wasn't interested in pursuing a relationship with me." Aiden's physical injuries were nothing compared with the pain from Maddie's rejection.

"I can also recognize the signs of a woman who's running away." Anna squeezed his arm. "Maybe your next challenge is to find out why."

Chapter Twenty-One

"Look at this, Miss M." Justin called Maddie over to the row of computers and motioned at the monitor. A photograph of a nylon backpack filled the screen.

"That doesn't look like an outline."

"I finished that a few minutes ago." Justin was too excited to respond to Maddie's teasing. "Aiden said I should order this one because it's the best. I'm going to get one for Tim for Christmas, too."

Maddie wondered how long it would be before her pulse didn't do a little hip-hop when someone said Aiden's name. "Are you and Tim planning to do some hiking?"

"Even better." Justin sat back in his chair. "Aiden is organizing a survival camping weekend for the church youth group in February. Tyler's going, too."

Tyler's wide grin confirmed it.

"So far it's guys only." Skye looked a little miffed. "If they can find some female chaperones, they'll make it coed."

"Maddie could come along," Justin suggested. "Three days in the wilderness. It's going to be sweet."

Skye's eyes lit up. "That's a great idea."

They were serious. Maddie would have been flattered

if the thought of spending a weekend with Aiden wasn't out of the question.

Out of the question, but oh so tempting.

"I'm sure they'll find a female chaperone." Once word got out that Aiden was in charge of the outing, Maddie knew there would be more volunteers than Pastor Seth knew what to do with. "Now, if everyone is finished with tonight's assignment, you're free to go. The rain is supposed to turn to sleet later this evening, and I don't want anyone driving home in bad weather."

Justin and Tyler, who'd started shoving things into their backpacks when Maddie said the words *free to go*, shot toward the door with a hasty goodbye.

Skye rolled her eyes. "If I have to listen to one more conversation about snow caves and vapor barriers, the next blooper reel is going public."

"They're excited." And Maddie was thrilled the teenagers had gotten involved with Pastor Seth's youth group. But the highlight of the week was when Justin had dragged a red-faced Tim up to the circulation desk to sign up for a library card.

A how-to with detailed drawings on building your own canoe was the first book the boy had checked out. Maddie could only assume it meant he'd been helping Liam in the shop.

"They're annoying," Skye countered. "And kind of cute when they're asleep in study hall."

Maddie chuckled. "I'll see you Friday."

Skye slipped on her coat. Halfway to the door, she turned around and jogged back to Maddie, extracting a flash drive from her purse. "I almost forgot! It's still pretty rough, but here are the first five minutes of my video collage. I wanted you to be the first one to see it."

The girl was gone before Maddie could respond.

She slipped the flash drive into the pocket of her corduroy jumper while she straightened up the media room. The wind had picked up outside, freezing rain spraying against the window like buckshot, making Maddie glad she'd sent the teenagers home early.

A peek outside at the deserted street told her it was safe to close the library a few minutes early, too.

She was about to shut down the computer when she remembered the flash drive.

The tiny stick, shaped like a bright orange Popsicle, should have elicited a smile, not a curl of apprehension.

Maddie was touched that Skye wanted her feedback, but she'd been trying to live in the here and now, not think about the past.

It's five minutes, Maddie chided herself. *You have to get over this. You and Aiden live in the same town.*

A town that seemed even smaller when you were trying to avoid someone.

She popped the drive into place, and the opening notes of the *Mission Impossible* theme fractured the silence.

Skye's sense of humor was one of the many reasons Maddie enjoyed spending time with her.

The video opened with Justin and Tyler's first safety lesson. Skye had captured the boys' tight grip on the canoe paddles—and on their emotions.

Maddie hadn't realized how terrified they'd been to step so far out of their comfort zone. She had been right there with Skye while she was recording the footage, but the story unfolding was more than two teenage boys training for a competition. She was seeing a friendship forming, too.

By the time the images of River Quest began to play, Maddie was riveted to the screen. The changes she saw in the boys were so dramatic, Maddie knew without a doubt that God was at work.

He was *still* at work.

And there was Aiden in the midst of it all, giving corrections and shouting encouragement from the sidelines.

It hurt to see him, and yet Maddie was so proud of the man he was. The man he would become now that he'd made peace with his past and with God.

The music changed, and another image popped up on the screen.

Maddie didn't know Skye had recorded *her*, too. Emerging from the smoke, torch in hand.

She remembered the smoke burning her lungs. The rushing sound in her ears.

What Maddie didn't remember was the smile on her face when she'd stumbled across the finish line a few seconds later.

The teenagers weren't the only ones who'd stepped out of their comfort zones. Her cheeks were flushed with color, hair trailing out the back of the baseball cap, a wild tangle of red and gold…

"You're beautiful."

Maddie whirled around.

"Aiden."

The man in the video had materialized behind her, as handsome and confident as the day he'd crashed her study session.

"Hi."

There you go, Aiden. Impress a librarian with your amazing ability to turn a one-syllable word into three.

But the speech he'd practiced all the way into town was gone. Erased. Deleted. Wiped away as his gaze bounced from the woman on the screen to the one standing in front of him.

Maddie tapped the mouse, and the music stopped. "What are you doing here?"

"I miss you."

Whoa. That hadn't been part of Aiden's speech, either, but the flash of longing in Maddie's eyes told him everything he needed to know.

In this instance, Aiden would have no trouble telling his family they were right. Maddie *did* have feelings for him.

"Have dinner with me tonight."

"Aiden…no."

"Why not?"

"I—I told you."

"You said we don't have anything in common, but that's not true." Aiden moved closer and pointed to the computer screen. "Because that girl, the one holding the torch, looks like she's having the time of her life."

Maddie moistened her lower lip. "I did."

"Then help me understand what I did to mess things up," Aiden said. "And I'll do whatever I can to fix it."

"You didn't do anything." Maddie looked stunned by the suggestion, putting another one of Aiden's fears to rest. "But it was one day, Aiden. You're talking about… more. I can't participate in all the things you enjoy. If a girl who enjoys paddling into whitewater rapids can't hold your interest past the first date, a girl who spends her free time curled up with a good book will bore you to tears."

Hold his interest past the first date?

The rumor mill had apparently rented out some space at the local library.

"I don't lead women on," Aiden said, struggling to keep his frustration in check. "And I'm *never* bored when I'm with you, Maddie. Whether we're looking at the stars or discussing the plot of *The Outsiders*, everything feels… right. I don't expect you to climb mountains or skydive. I did some research on heart conditions, and I'd *never* ask you to do anything that might compromise your health." He took a chance. Took her hand.

"When you were doing your research," Maddie began

slowly, "you must have read about complications during pregnancy."

Aiden's next breath seized in his lungs. All he could do was shake his head.

"I found out when I was sixteen that I was in the high-risk category. Every situation is unique, but the doctor made it very clear that a family isn't…isn't in my future."

Aiden's heart broke for her.

"Maddie…you should have told me."

"When?" Her voice cracked on the word. "When is a good time to tell a man something like that, Aiden? The first time you meet him? After you've been dating a few months? Or do you wait until you're falling in love and you pray it won't matter even though you know it will?"

Maddie wondered if Aiden even realized he'd let go of her hand.

She folded her arms across her chest, tucking them under her elbows to take away the chill.

Aiden had asked for the truth, and now he had to be honest with himself. In spite of everything he'd just said, did he still want to be with her?

"I know this might change things," Maddie said quietly. "And I understand if you need some time to think about it."

"I—" Aiden's lips flattened. "I'm sorry, Maddie."

She could feel tears pushing up into her throat, but she managed to hold them at bay until he'd left the room.

At least now he understood why she'd turned him down. Maddie looked at the girl on the computer screen one last time before she shut it down and walked to the front of the library. She had to straighten up the children's area and empty the coffeepot in the reading nook.

But someone already had. And that someone was sprawled in a chair holding a coffee cup.

"I—I thought you left."

"You told me to take some time." Aiden smiled, even though tears still glistened in his eyes. "So I did."

It was impossible for Maddie to move. Not with the soles of her ballet flats stuck to the floor.

Aiden set the cup down and rose to his feet. Padded over to her. "Do you want to know what I concluded?"

Maddie's knees turned to liquid when Aiden drew her into his arms. "W-what?"

"Yes, I've always wanted a family. And the God of the Universe knew that a man who's adopted would be open to children who share his name, even if they don't share his DNA."

The tears Maddie had tried so hard to hold at bay began to stream down her cheeks.

"You can't make a decision like that on an impulse," she whispered. "I've watched you with the twins and with Justin and Tyler. You're going to be a great dad. I don't expect you to close the door on something so important to you."

"I'm not," Aiden said. "And there's nothing impulsive about it. Adoption was something God put in my heart the day Sunni signed the papers that made us a family." He tipped her chin up until there was nowhere to look but in his incredible blue eyes. "If anything has changed in the last fifteen minutes, it's that I'm even more convinced that God brought us together. I'm in love with you, Maddie. Life doesn't come with guarantees, but God promises that He'll always be with us—something you reminded me of."

He loved her.

Maddie closed her eyes, sure this was a dream. But when she opened them, Aiden was still there.

Giving her the courage to say the words, too.

"I love you, too, Aiden. But—"

He pressed his finger against her lips. "No *buts*. We know our starting place, and we know our destination. What happens in between...that's what makes it an adventure. And just for the record—" Aiden's fingers traced the curve of Maddie's jaw and found the sensitive spot behind her ear "—tonight would be our *fifth* date."

"Fifth?" The word came out a little wobbly.

"Uh-huh. On our first date, we snuggled together in the conference room—"

"You sat next to me while I took notes!" Laughter bubbled up inside Maddie, and she remembered what her mom had said.

If you find a man who makes you laugh...

Aiden did that and so much more. He made her believe there could be another ending to the story she'd written.

"I'm counting it," Aiden said firmly. "Our second date was a romantic drive in the woods. Then we had dinner together—with my entire family and a bunch of teenagers, but still—and after that we sat underneath the stars. I remember thinking the Andromeda Galaxy wasn't nearly as fascinating as the woman sitting next to me." Aiden was teasing a strand of hair that had worked its way free from Maddie's bun now. "Which brings us to number five. The night when I walk you to your door and kiss you goodnight."

Maddie's heart just about leaped out of her chest.

"Unless you think I'm moving too fast." For the first time, Aiden looked a little uncertain.

Maddie peeked at him through her lashes. "Actually... I was thinking you don't have to wait that long."

Aiden's lips hitched in a smile and he drew her closer, claimed her lips with a heady combination of tenderness and passion that reflected the man who'd captured her heart.

Life with Aiden would be an adventure.

And here...in his arms...was a wonderful place to start.

Epilogue

Aiden tossed the ball into the air and caught it again.

"I'm not sure how it started, but a friendly game of football on the day of the first snowfall is a Kane family tradition."

"I know how it started." Sunni's eyes sparkled with laughter. "There were three boys wrestling on the kitchen floor while I was trying to make dinner. I shooed them outside and told them to work up an appetite."

Liam sidled up and snagged the football out of Aiden's hands. "But then Mom saw how much fun we were having and decided to join in."

"The real reason," Sunni said in a pseudo-whisper, "was to prevent a trip to the ER. I figured the boys would mind their manners if an old lady had the ball."

Maddie wasn't sure if it was Sunni referring to herself as old or describing Aiden and his brothers as boys that had her struggling to hide a smile.

"That's why Maddie agreed to act as our official referee." Aiden didn't try to steal the ball back as he sauntered over to her side and wrapped both his arms around her waist.

The scars around his eye had faded, but with the two days' growth of stubble on his jaw, Aiden still looked a little like the pirate who'd limped through the door of the library on that crisp September morning.

Cassie and Chloe slid up to Liam, bundled in matching coats and colorful scarves. Maddie had been encouraged to dress for the weather, too, so she'd chosen a hand-knit sweater, fleece leggings and the pair of thick-soled camouflage boots Aiden had given her the week before.

"Not the most romantic gift," he'd said when Maddie opened the package.

Maybe not—but the kiss that followed had been ten times warmer than the boots' Thinsulate liners.

"Maddie?"

With a start, Maddie realized Sunni had been speaking to her.

"I'm sorry," she stammered. "I was..."

"Distracted by my mesmerizing blue eyes," Aiden said.

Maddie elbowed him in the ribs. Even though he was right.

"I'd tell Aiden not to tease you, but I've learned it comes with the territory," Lily said. "You'll get used to it."

Maddie was not only getting used to it, she was thoroughly enjoying Aiden's family. She loved watching him interact with his brothers. Loved the laughter and the good-natured teasing and the way everyone looked out for each other.

"All I said was that I'm going up to the house to check on dinner and I'll be back in a few minutes." Sunni handed Maddie the whistle. "So I'm leaving you in charge."

After she bustled away, Maddie whispered, "You do realize I know nothing about football."

"That's okay." Aiden winked at her. "We're not very good at following the rules anyway."

Dodger abandoned his game of tag with Missy and bounded over, tail wagging, a black glove Maddie recognized as belonging to Aiden clamped between his teeth.

"I was wondering where that went." Aiden held out his hand. "Hand it over."

"Are you ready to play, too?" Maddie bent down and scratched the dog's prickly fur.

Dodger spun in a circle, churning up a sparkling cloud of freshly fallen snow.

"I guess that means yes." Aiden tugged on the glove. "You're defense."

"Need a helmet, Aiden?" Brendan jogged past them with a grin. "So you don't mess up that pretty face again?"

"Maddie? Don't blow the whistle yet."

"Why not?"

"Because I'm going to tackle my big brother, and tackling isn't allowed in touch football." Aiden bounded after Brendan.

Lily slipped her arm around Maddie's shoulders and smiled. "You'll get used to this, too."

Aiden watched the twins grab Maddie's hands as everyone filed into the house an hour later. Her cheeks and the tip of her nose were pink, and she was laughing at something Cassie was saying.

His heart felt so incredibly *full.*

Thank you, God.

Maddie, who'd once described herself as an outsider, had already become part of his family. Now was the time to make it official.

As they passed the sunroom, Aiden steered Maddie into the sunroom and closed the door.

"Aiden." Her throaty chuckle had a dangerous effect on his heart. "What are you doing?"

"Kidnapping you for a minute."

"Of course you are." She melted against him, a willing prisoner.

Aiden pressed a lingering kiss on Maddie's lips, one that took up the entire sixty seconds of that minute.

"Your family is waiting for us," she murmured when they finally broke apart.

"One more minute." Aiden drew her over to the couch. "I have something for you."

"*Aiden.* You're spoiling me."

"I like spoiling you." And the blush on Maddie's cheeks was one of the reasons why. "Now, if Dodger didn't find this first..." He reached underneath the coffee table and pulled out a brown paper sack. The handles were tied together with what looked like binder twine but was, according to the clerk at the store where Aiden had purchased it, something called raffia.

Maddie burrowed through the tissue paper, and when her eyes went wide, Aiden knew she'd already guessed the contents.

"My favorite book," he said when she drew it from the bag. "And I hope it will be yours, too."

Maddie opened the cover and smiled. "Um... Aiden? There's nothing written in it."

"That's because it's *our* story," he said. "And I know it's going to be pretty great." Aiden watched Maddie run her fingers over the butter-soft leather. "Do you like it?"

"I love it."

"Good. Because there's more."

"Aiden!"

He grinned. "I saw it and thought of you."

"You said the same thing about the boots. And the camera."

"Someone has to document all the awesome things God has in store for us. Now close your eyes," Aiden instructed. "I didn't have time to wrap this one."

Maddie obeyed. Aiden eased onto one knee beside the sofa, hands shaking so much he almost dropped the tiny velvet box he'd stashed in his pocket. "Okay." Maddie opened her eyes. Aiden saw the split second of confusion when she realized he wasn't beside her change to wonder when she saw the ring in his hand.

"Aiden..." She breathed his name and the tears that sprang into her eyes made Aiden forget the proposal he'd rehearsed.

"I love you, Maddie. If it's too soon, you can tell me. I'm not going anywhere. But I wanted you to know that I'm ready to start our life together. The sunrises and sunsets and whatever happens in between."

"Yes." Maddie laughed, tears streaming down her face, and held out her hand. "Yes. Yes. Yes."

"I told you that's what Miss Maddie would say," someone whispered outside the door.

"She's going to be Aunt Maddie now, Chloe."

Aiden shook his head, but Maddie smiled.

"Aunt Maddie," she repeated. "I like the sound of that."

Aiden pulled her into his arms again. "How do you feel about Mrs. Kane?"

Maddie pressed a kiss against Aiden's lips. "I like that even better."

"Aiden picked this out himself?" Brendan inspected the ring and gave Maddie a quick wink before he turned to Aiden. "Not bad, little brother."

Maddie knew Brendan was teasing but she happened to think the princess-cut diamond, centered with two green stones on a delicate filigree brand, was perfect.

I know emeralds aren't traditional, Aiden had said. *But the color matches your eyes.*

And the man who'd slipped the ring on Maddie's finger was her perfect match.

The celebration of their engagement had taken priority over the first snowfall.

Sunni had baked a two-layer cake with drifts of buttercream frosting for dessert, but the red confetti hearts sprinkled over the top made Maddie suspect that Aiden's mom had known about the proposal before the twins had scampered back to the living room and broken the news.

She'd also suggested Maddie invite her parents over to celebrate with them, so when the doorbell rang a few minutes later, Aiden leaped to his feet.

"I'll get it." He winked at Maddie. "I have to win my future in-laws over."

Maddie smiled, knowing he already had. As it turned out, Aiden was an accomplished chess player and had insisted on spending Saturday evenings with her parents over the past month.

Aiden returned a few minutes later—alone—and the expression on his face brought Maddie to her feet.

"Wayne just delivered this." Aiden held up an envelope. "It's a certified letter from a law office—on behalf of the Holt-McIntyre Agency."

Maddie started praying as the family gathered around him. She knew Brendan had contacted the agency a few days after she'd relayed the information Trish had shared, but there'd been no response.

A month had passed since then, and the continued silence had weighed on everyone. Maddie knew Aiden had been hoping the next communication would be a phone call from his sister, not a letter from an attorney.

"Bren?" Aiden looked at his oldest brother, but Brendan shook his head.

"Go ahead." His voice was husky.

Maddie slipped her arm around Aiden's waist and felt the tremor that rippled down his spine.

"In regard to your recent petition..." He read the opening paragraph, a polite response to the letter Brendan had sent to the adoption agency, explaining the unique circumstances of their situation.

The second paragraph was couched in legalese and reiterated that both parties had believed they were acting in the best interests of the child when they agreed to a closed adoption.

"My client is currently out of the country and cannot be reached at this time. After she returns, I will make a recommendation based on the information you've provided. Sincerely, Jameson Ford."

"*He'll* make a recommendation?" Liam echoed. "What is that supposed to mean?"

Brendan slipped his arm around Lily's waist. "It's out of our hands now."

"But not God's." Aiden drew Maddie against his side. "Someone reminded me recently that we can't focus on the *ifs*. Whatever happens in the future, we can trust Him."

Maddie pressed closer to the man she loved, thanking God with all her heart because it was true.

* * * * *

Dear Reader,

I hope you enjoyed your latest visit to Castle Falls! Like for Maddie, books were a constant companion while I was growing up and I spent hours in my hometown library. The librarian's three-book rule never applied to me—she knew that I would read all of them on the walk home and always let me check out more!

When I was a teenager, that same librarian introduced me to an author named Grace Livingston Hill, who wrote sweet, faith-filled romances. Those books touched my heart and sparked a lifelong love for happily-ever-after endings that continues in the stories that I write.

Sunni Mason, Aiden's adoptive mom, plays matchmaker to her three sons, but I think that librarians do a little matchmaking, too! They bring books and the people who love them together. The next time you visit your local library, be sure to thank them!

I would love to hear from you! Please visit my website at kathrynspringer.com and drop me a note or check out my Facebook page at kathrynspringerauthor.

Walk in joy!
Kathryn Springer

COMING NEXT MONTH FROM
Love Inspired®

Available April 17, 2018

THE WEDDING QUILT BRIDE
Brides of Lost Creek • by Marta Perry

Widowed single mom Rebecca Mast returns to her Amish community hoping to open a quilt shop. She accepts carpenter Daniel King's offer of assistance—but she isn't prepared for the bond he forms with her son. Will getting closer expose her secret—or reveal the love she has in her heart for her long-ago friend?

THE AMISH WIDOW'S NEW LOVE
by Liz Tolsma

To raise money for her infant son's surgery, young Amish widow Naomi Miller must work with Elam Yoder—the man she once hoped to wed before he ran off. Elam's back seeking forgiveness—and a second chance with the woman he could never forget.

THE RANCHER'S SECRET CHILD
Bluebonnet Springs • by Brenda Minton

Marcus Palermo's simple life gets complicated when he meets the son he never knew he had—and his beautiful guardian. Lissa Hart thought she'd only stick around long enough to aid Marcus in becoming a dad—but could her happily-ever-after lie with the little boy and the rugged rancher?

HER TEXAS COWBOY
by Jill Lynn

Still nursing a broken heart since Rachel Maddox left town—and him—years earlier, rancher next door Hunter McDermott figures he can at least be cordial during her brief return. But while they work together on the Independence Day float, he realizes it's impossible to follow through on his plan because he's never stopped picturing her as his wife.

HOMETOWN REUNION
by Lisa Carter

Returning home, widowed former Green Beret Jaxon Pruitt is trying to put down roots and reconnect with his son. Though he took over the kayak shop his childhood friend Darcy Parks had been saving for, she shows him how to bond with little Brody—and finds herself wishing to stay with them forever.

AN UNEXPECTED FAMILY
Maple Springs • by Jenna Mindel

Cam Zelinsky never imagined himself as a family man—especially after making some bad choices in his life. But in seeking redemption, he volunteers to help single mom Rose Dean save her diner—and soon sees she and her son are exactly who he needs for a happy future.

LOOK FOR THESE AND OTHER LOVE INSPIRED BOOKS WHEREVER BOOKS ARE SOLD, INCLUDING MOST BOOKSTORES, SUPERMARKETS, DISCOUNT STORES AND DRUGSTORES.

LICNM0418

Widowed single mom Rebecca Mast returns to her Amish community hoping to open a quilt shop. She accepts carpenter Daniel King's offer of assistance—but she isn't prepared for the bond he forms with her son. Will getting closer expose her secret—or reveal the love she has in her heart for her long-ago friend?

Read on for a sneak preview of
THE WEDDING QUILT BRIDE
by Marta Perry,
available May 2018 from Love Inspired!

"Do you want to make decisions about the rest of the house today, or just focus on the shop for now?"

"Just the shop today," Rebecca said quickly. "It's more important than getting moved in right away."

"If I know your *mamm* and *daad*, they'd be happy to have you stay with them in the *grossdaadi* house for always, ain't so?"

"That's what they say, but we shouldn't impose on them."

"Impose? Since when is it imposing to have you home again? Your folks have been so happy since they knew you were coming. You're not imposing," Daniel said.

Rebecca stiffened, seeming to put some distance between them. "It's better that I stand on my own feet. I'm not a girl any longer." She looked as if she might want to add that it wasn't his business.

No, it wasn't. And she certain sure wasn't the girl he remembered. Grief alone didn't seem enough to account for the changes in her. Had there been some other problem, something he didn't know about in her time away or in her marriage?

He'd best mind his tongue and keep his thoughts on business, he told himself. He was the last person to know anything about marriage, and that was the way he wanted it. Or if not wanted, he corrected honestly, at least the way it had to be.

"I guess we should get busy measuring for all these things, so I'll know what I'm buying when I go to the mill." Pulling out his steel measure, he focused on the boy. "Mind helping me by holding one end of this, Lige?"

The boy hesitated for a moment, studying him as if looking at the question from all angles. Then he nodded, taking a few steps toward Daniel, who couldn't help feeling a little spurt of triumph.

Daniel held out an end of the tape. "If you'll hold this end right here on the corner, I'll measure the whole wall. Then we can see how many racks we'll be able to put up."

Daniel measured, checking a second time before writing the figures down in his notebook. His gaze slid toward Lige again. It wondered him how the boy came to be so quiet and solemn. He certain sure wasn't like his *mammi* had been when she was young. Could be he was still having trouble adjusting to his *daadi*'s dying, he supposed.

Rebecca was home, but he sensed she had brought some troubles with her. As for him…well, he didn't have answers. He just had a lot of questions.

LIEXP0418